The Blind Date

Book 1 of the *Love Unexpected* series

Delaney Diamond

Chapter One

Shawna Ferguson was late. Very late. And she hated being late because she valued people's time the same way she wanted them to value hers.

Bottom line, she'd have to bite the bullet and buy a new car, no matter how much she dreaded the car-buying process. Her once dependable Corolla was no longer dependable now that it was on its last leg.

She hurried to the front door of her favorite French restaurant, the heels of her Manolo Blahniks hitting the pavement hard with each stride. She pulled her camel-colored wrap sweater tighter over her sleeveless dress to protect against the chill in the air. It was early spring, that time of year when the days were warm but the nights were cool, and the best way to protect against the changes in temperature meant dressing in layers.

A blind date.

Why had she agreed to this? For some reason she'd listened to her older sister, Yvonne, and decided to take the plunge back into the dating pool, even though her luck with men seemed to have run out months ago.

The three-day-old conversation with Yvonne about tonight's date replayed in her head.

****

Yvonne Wallace looked at Shawna from across the table in the kitchen. They were having breakfast, and as usual, Little Miss Homemaker—as Shawna liked to teasingly call her sister—had set out a feast of homemade raisin bread, butter and homemade jam, scrambled eggs, and fruit cups.

Only two years separated the sisters, but their personalities were as different as black and white. While Shawna had dreamed of opening her own boutique, which she'd accomplished four years ago, Yvonne had dreamed of becoming a wife and mother. At twenty-four she'd married a doctor, and by their second anniversary, she'd quit her job to make that dream a reality. After six years of marriage, they had a four-year-old daughter and two-year-old son, and Yvonne was seven months pregnant with her second son. Taking care of her family and getting ready for the baby filled her days.

Yvonne was one of those people who, because she was happily married, wanted the same for everyone else. She'd found her Mr. Right and claimed he existed for every woman. Shawna knew better. Finding a good man—with whom one was compatible—seemed as unrealistic as finding a diamond mine on her property. Basically, it wasn't gonna happen, and Shawna had resigned herself to the fact.

Her sister couldn't seem to understand she was perfectly happy being single, and she kept trying to help Shawna find a man through "chance" meetings and "unexpected" visits when Shawna came to visit her.

When the conversation came up about her paltry dating options, Shawna had a solution. "I'll hire an escort the next time I need to attend an event with a date." She shrugged.

"Ew. You will not. No sister of mine is going to pay for a date."

"There's nothing nasty about it," Shawna said. "Lots of women do it nowadays."

"Desperate women."

"*No.* Women who don't have the time or energy to sift through what's out there. The companies match you up with someone who has similar interests, you go out, and then you're done. Bam. No fuss, no muss."

"Why do that when I have the perfect man for you?"

"I'm not looking for a man."

Yvonne rolled her eyes. "Okay, whatever. I have the perfect *escort* for you. Is that better?"

"No offense, but you haven't exactly done a good job setting me up with the right men in the past." Shawna pretended to be in deep thought. "Let's see, remember the guy from your church, Steve, who started singing hymns in the car on the ride back home and prayed for my soul as we stood at the front door?"

"He loves the Lord. What's wrong with that?"

Shawna narrowed her eyes and continued. "David, who wouldn't stop talking about his ex-wife the entire night. Our date ended with him crying on my shoulder about how much he missed her."

"Look at the bright side. You got a free meal, and at least you didn't waste any more time with him than necessary. One date in and you already knew he was wrong for you."

"And I can't forget Nolan. Sexy, suave, rich. What a surprise to see his face on the evening news as the person who'd robbed several banks in the area and left lines of poetry as his trademark. Just think, I can say I dated the Poetry Bandit."

"Granted, I should have dug a little deeper when he said he worked in banking."

Shawna sighed. "I know you mean well, but your choice in men leaves me a bit . . . how should I say this? Terrified." Shawna slathered butter on the bread and bit into a crunchy slice.

"This guy could be right for you, though. I really think the two of you will hit it off."

"How do you know him?"

"So you're interested?"

"Answer the question."

"He's a friend of William's."

The fact that he was one of her brother-in-law's friends meant he was probably better vetted than the men her sister had introduced her to in the past. Interest piqued, she said, "Tell me about him."

"I thought you weren't interested."

"Would you tell me about him!"

Yvonne giggled, cocky in her triumph. "Like I said, William knows him better, but I've also met him, and he's really nice. You'll like him."

~ 4 ~

"What does he look like?"

"He's about six feet tall. Great personality, really nice guy."

Shawna watched her sister closely. She seemed evasive, which made Shawna suspicious. "You mentioned nice twice, but not whether or not he's attractive. Does he have an eye in the middle of his forehead or something?"

Yvonne waved her hand and snorted, as if to say, *don't be ridiculous.* "Of course not."

"Then what does he look like?"

"Don't worry, he's attractive. He's not your usual type, that's all. So please don't do that thing you do."

"What thing?" Shawna asked, already offended.

"You know that thing you do when you're trying to cover up your surprise or when you don't like something—you smile, but it's this weird, creepy smile. Be open-minded."

"I don't do that. And why would I need to be open-minded? What's wrong with him, Yvonne?" Concern started to set in.

"Nothing. But really, I don't want to spoil the surprise. Trust your big sister on this one, okay?"

****

So she'd trusted her sister and shown up here to meet a complete stranger.

When Shawna entered the restaurant, smiling staff welcomed her with a *"Bienvenue!"* She told the hostess she had a reservation and gave her the name of the person with whom she had the meeting. "Roger James."

"Your party's already here." The brunette

smiled, and her gaze drifted to the interior wall, outside Shawna's line of vision.

Shawna pasted a smile on her face and stepped forward to get a good look. That's when her date stepped from the dim interior into the better-lit entryway.

Her smile froze in place and her body became as stiff as a corpse.

It wasn't that her date was unattractive. Oh no, he didn't suffer from a deficiency in looks at all. In fact, he was sexy. Hella sexy. Even more sexy than the last time she'd seen him, though a bit underdressed in a pair of jeans and a button-down shirt with the sleeves rolled up to reveal rugged arms dusted with fine hair. Wisps of dark hair, which she knew from firsthand experience were soft, brushed the collar of his striped shirt.

She pressed her palm to her chest in a futile attempt to control the erratic beat of her heart. Unfortunately, her brain had gone into overdrive, reminding her of unbridled passion in Chicago six years ago when she'd fallen into bed with this man.

She'd never forgotten the two torrid nights they'd spent together where the intimacies they shared had left her breathless and exhausted in his arms. Every caress of his lips and touch of his rough, work-worn hands was seared into her brain. And she could never, ever forget what it felt like to have the dark stubble shadowing his jaw graze the sensitive spot on her neck—or the skin of her inner thigh.

Her knees weakened at the thought.

A corner of his lips did a slow slant upward,

and Shawna tore her eyes away from the invitation in them to stare into a pair of amazing blue eyes that rooted her in place.

"Hello, Shawna." The mellow sound of his voice greeted her as he approached. He exuded a confidence and casual virility not present during their first introduction. Back then, he'd been a little less sure of himself, though very charming.

The sound of her name on his tongue sent a tremor through every cell of her body. "Ryan." She whispered his name in disbelief because his name wasn't Roger James, and he wasn't a stranger. She'd hoped never to set eyes on this man again.

"It's good to see you, love."

Shocked out of her reverie by the affectionate word, rage erupted inside of Shawna. She hadn't seen him since that day in Chicago when her heart had shattered into a thousand pieces. She did what she hadn't been able to do back then.

She hauled back and slapped him.

Chapter Two

Ryan touched his throbbing cheek. "I deserved that."

"Damn right you did," Shawna said. She swung away from him and the open-mouthed hostess and stormed out of the restaurant.

"Shawna, wait!"

A few steps outside the door, he caught up with her and grasped her arm.

"Let go of me." She pulled away. "Is this your idea of a joke? How did you get my sister to agree to this?"

"She didn't know. I told her and William we had a few dates in Chicago, and I wanted to surprise you."

"Well, I'm surprised."

"I thought it was the only way I could get you to see me. I figured if you knew you were meeting me, you'd never agree to it."

"So you stooped to your old tricks of telling

lies, Ryan? Old habits die hard, don't they?"

He winced.

A barrage of emotions raced through her. She wished she could slap him again, but she'd had the element of surprise on her side the first time. She didn't think it would work a second time.

"Come back inside. Let's talk."

"I have nothing to say to you."

They stared at each other. The spring temperature couldn't cool Shawna's heated skin or her hot temper. Ryan was the last person she ever wanted to see again. Too bad he looked so good. Had he actually gotten better looking? Why couldn't he have started balding or developed a paunch—something, *any*thing to make him pay for what he'd done.

"Shawna, please. At least let me buy you dinner. For old times' sake."

She turned her back on him and closed her eyes. *Old times' sake.*

Why did seeing him tear her apart like this? She hated him after what he'd done. He'd used her.

"No." *Walk away, Shawna.*

"Why not? It wasn't all bad, was it?"

And that was the problem. Before she found out the truth, the time they'd spent together had been good. That's why their break up—could she even call it that since they hadn't been in a relationship?—had been so devastating.

"You shouldn't have done this, Ryan," she said in a low voice.

"It was six years ago." The exterior lights cast shadows on the ground in the darkness so she saw him when he moved closer. "I would think," he said, his voice equally low behind her, "that after six years, you could find a way to . . . I don't know . . ." He sighed. "I don't expect forgiveness. I know what I did was wrong, but we had something. Didn't we?"

He moved in front of her, and she had no choice but to look at him. It brought him into such close proximity that she could smell his cologne. The same scent, containing hints of sandalwood and vanilla. It brought back even more memories. She looked him in the eyes, standing only a couple of inches shorter in her heels. She maintained eye contact despite the tremor in her belly.

"No," she replied. "We had the opposite of something. *Nothing*. Because you thought it fine to play games."

"I wasn't playing games."

"What would you call it then? Having your cake and eating it, too?"

Ryan ran his hand over his dark brown hair. "I wouldn't call it that, either."

"You used me."

"*No.*" His mouth set in a grim line, he stepped close. "That was never my intention. You have to believe me. Can we sit down and talk? We're both already here."

She shook her head, not only to deny him but also to clear it.

"Do you want me to beg?" He lowered his voice. "Have dinner with me. You know you want to stay, no matter how much you despise me. I know how much you enjoy French food, and William said this is your favorite restaurant. That's why I picked this place."

He'd remembered how much she loved French food. But would it really only be dinner? It hadn't been that first night.

The corners of his mouth twitched, and she fought the urge to give in to the temptation chipping away at her resolve. She glanced back at the door. "This *is* my favorite restaurant."

She'd started the downward slide into dangerous territory, justifying why it should be okay to sit down and have dinner with a man whose presence had her tangled in knots. Who, as he said, she should despise, but couldn't because of a different emotion which she refused to acknowledge.

He touched her arm above her elbow, and she pulled away from him. "No touching."

He lifted his hands in surrender. "No touching," he agreed.

They eyed each other. She wavered, and he waited. She remained quiet, hesitant, and he waited.

The urge to walk away was weaker than her curiosity. She wanted to hear what he had to say and find out how he'd been over the years.

"Appetizers and drinks only," she said, feeling the need to state conditions so she'd have some level of control over the way the evening progressed.

"No problem." The lazy smile she'd become familiar with in Chicago returned. It made him look as if he had a secret he relished keeping to himself.

"I mean it."

"I'm not arguing."

Shawna tossed another hard look his way before she stalked back into the restaurant ahead of him. The hostess smiled a greeting when she saw them, giving no indication she'd seen them in an altercation minutes ago.

They followed the young woman into the dim interior toward their reserved table. Ryan brought up the rear. She felt his hot gaze on the back of her head, and it took great effort to walk steadily across the carpeted floor.

The dim lights and candles gave the impression of warmth and coziness in the large restaurant. The mouth-watering aroma of heavy sauces and fresh herbs reminded Shawna why she loved this place.

She'd been here many times before, but she never grew tired of the food, the ambiance, or the Parisian landmarks painted on the walls. The images brought back memories of the summer she spent in France and the rented room above the bakery where she'd spent the best three months of her life.

There was the Eiffel Tower, the Arc de Triomphe at the end of the Champs-Élysées, and the Sacré-Cœur Basilica, located at the highest point in the city. If she wasn't so upset about seeing Ryan, she'd sigh with nostalgia like she always did.

"Your server will be with you in a minute," the hostess said.

Ryan couldn't take his eyes off Shawna.

What were the chances that William Wallace's

sister-in-law was Shawna Ferguson? He'd met William at a local bar and they'd become friends, meeting up every so often to drink beer and debate politics, argue over sports, or bemoan their problems with the fairer sex. Sometimes all of the above. During all that time, he'd had no idea they were related and had only found out a few weeks ago.

When William had mentioned the name Shawna, and at Ryan's request followed up with a photo of his sister-in-law, Ryan had stopped breathing, unable to believe his luck. She'd been in his thoughts numerous times over the years, and he'd given up any chance of ever seeing her again.

Now, here she sat, across from him.

She had bangs now, and the overhead light picked up the reddish tones in the dark brown strands, reminding him of the colorful striations in the cherry wood at his woodworking shop. Reminding him, too, of how he'd wound his fingers in her hair to hold her in place while he drove into her.

With her hair pulled back into a neat ponytail, he could drink in her features. Physically, she hadn't changed over the years. Smooth, dark skin, a somewhat pointy nose, and her mouth . . . It had been the first thing he noticed when he'd gotten close enough to see her features that first day. Pouty, generous. The kind of mouth a man wanted to take his time kissing.

So many parts of her were generous. Her breasts, for example, which he now had a good view of because she'd removed her sweater. The material of the short-sleeved dress looked like it had been melted over them, prominently displaying the luscious mounds in all their glory.

He shifted in the chair to alleviate the tightening in his pants.

Then of course, there was her generous behind, which he'd enjoyed seeing, whether covered in a pair of tight jeans or when he'd had the pleasure of watching her slip from the hotel bed to the bathroom. He couldn't decide which view he liked best—watching her coming or going.

A pair of sultry brown eyes beneath long lashes looked up at him from the menu. "Do you know what you want?"

Ryan leaned back in the chair, keeping his gaze on her. He hated the way they'd parted, but he had no one to blame but himself. He'd been young, foolish, and a coward.

"Yes. I know exactly what I want."

From the moment he'd seen her, he'd known.

Chapter Three

Chicago, Friday, six years ago

From his position at the end of the aisle at the Food Mart, Ryan watched the young black woman at the other end flip through a magazine. She looked a couple of years younger than his twenty-four.

Impeccable in a blue dress that showed off her hourglass figure, she had a Coach purse hung over one shoulder and wore a pair of patent leather pumps shiny enough to double as a mirror. Her dark brown, shoulder-length hair looked lustrous and silky, covering most of her face. Lucky for him, he'd seen her when she first walked in and had received the full effect.

Other than a quick glance, she hadn't paid attention to him, but he couldn't say the same. He'd been watching her ever since she entered the store and had yet to work up the nerve to approach.

Shaking his head, he walked away.

He wasn't exactly dressed to impress, unshaven in an old T-shirt, worn jeans, and a baseball cap turned backwards. She'd probably take one look at him and laugh.

Ryan went two aisles over and picked up the toiletries he'd come in to purchase and then headed for the check-out. At the front, he saw her standing in line. He went to the other cashier and waited behind an elderly woman with a cane, counting out her payment in quarters.

The young black woman laughed and said something to the male cashier. He couldn't hear what she'd said, but he'd heard her laugh well enough, and he liked the sound of it. From his sideways grin, it looked like the cashier was flirting with her.

Ryan looked at the elderly woman beside him. Her wrinkled fingers trembled as she counted.

"One, two, three, four—four dollars. One, two, three, four—five dollars."

He and the cashier made eye contact, and the young woman smiled apologetically.

His gaze shifted again, and he saw the object of his attention had finished her purchase and headed on her way out the door.

"One, two, three, four—seven dollars."

A wave of panic seized him. He couldn't let her walk away. He had to take the chance, even if he risked being laughed at. Besides, if she brushed him off, soon he'd be back in Oklahoma and would never see her again.

"One, two, three, four—nine dollars."

What did he have to lose?

"Sorry," Ryan muttered to the cashier. "I'll be back to get those." Abandoning his items on the conveyor belt, he turned sideways and slid past the senior citizen, rushing to the revolving door.

Outside, he looked left down Michigan Avenue, then right—and that's when he saw her. Heart racing, he quickened his steps and walked up beside her. "Hi."

"Hi," she said cautiously.

"I don't usually do this, and I wish I'd thought of a line before I approached you, but I . . . I saw you and followed you and wanted to meet you."

She kept walking, but a small smile hovered around her mouth. "Is that right?"

"Yeah."

"I saw you, too."

"You did?" Progress already. He couldn't help the grin that spread across his face. "What did you think?"

"I thought the whole hat to the back thing doesn't work unless you're a hip-hop artist or in a boy band."

"Ouch. That hurt." He twisted the brim of his hat to the front. "What else?"

"Are you really following me?"

"I've been following you since we were in the Food Mart."

"Should I be worried?"

"I'm harmless."

She looked him up and down but didn't say a word. They walked along in silence. He'd acted before thinking, and he rummaged through his brain to think of what to say next.

"What's your name?" he asked.

"You first."

"Ryan Stewart."

"Shawna."

"I'll never forget that name. Do you have a last name?"

"Yes, but I'm not giving it to you." They slowed to a stop in front of Saks Fifth Avenue. "Well, Ryan Stewart, as flattering as it is to have a man follow me from the Food Mart, I have to go now. My lunch break's over, and I have to get back to work."

Ryan stuffed his hands in his pockets. "What do you do here?" he asked, trying to prolong their time together. "If I wanted to get a gift for someone, would you be the person to speak to?"

"I could help, but you'd be better off talking to one of the seasoned sales reps. I'm finishing up my summer job here, and I work in visual merchandising."

"Summer job? Do you live in Chicago, or . . . ?"

"I'm a Southern girl, and I . . . look, I have to go. It was really sweet of you to say hello."

"Have dinner with me," he blurted as she turned away.

Her eyebrows lifted in surprise. "Are you serious?"

"As a hostage situation."

Her eyes darted away so he couldn't read her thoughts. A light breeze blew hair across her face, and he almost reached up to brush away the fine strands that caressed her cheek and wrapped around her neck. She tucked the fluttering strands behind her ear.

Her brow furrowed. "Why me?" she asked.

"Out of all these women walking around out here."

"There are other women out here?" Ryan looked around at the pedestrians as if seeing them for the first time. "I didn't even notice. I only have eyes for you."

A beat later, they both burst out laughing.

"Good one," Shawna said. "Have you used it before?"

"First time. I thought of it on the fly. Good though, right?" He stopped grinning and looked her in the eyes to make sure she knew how serious he was. "But I meant it. Let me buy you dinner."

"Ryan, I'm not interested in seeing anyone right now. You seem very sweet, but I'll be leaving in a couple of days, so I don't think this is a good idea."

He couldn't let her get away. She had to say yes. He'd come to Chicago to clear his head, and somehow he knew she'd play an important role in helping him finalize the decision he'd been struggling to make.

"It's only dinner." He could see her waver as she shifted from one foot to the other and tucked her purse closer to her body. "When do you get off?"

She laughed nervously. "This is ridiculous."

"No, it's not. You have to eat and I want to feed you. Makes sense to me." He hoped that by keeping the conversation light, she wouldn't overthink it and slip from his grasp, leaving him standing there with no way to see her again. "What kind of food do you like?"

Shawna shook her head in defeat. "French cuisine is my favorite."

"And when do you get off?"

"At six."

"I'll be here at five-fifty, waiting."

"If you're not, it's no big deal." She shrugged.

He fixed his gaze on her face. "I hope that's not true."

She hesitated, tilting her head slightly, brown eyes observing him as if trying to figure him out. She obviously still doubted his sincerity.

"I'll see you at six, Ryan Stewart."

Chapter Four

Present day, Atlanta

Somehow, Ryan had charmed Shawna into accepting his invitation to dinner that day. She could tell some of the charm was still there, though she noted differences in him that came with age. He still had an easygoing, affable personality, but his face had matured and he had bigger muscles, causing him to exude an overt masculinity that called out to her femininity.

She closed her menu when the waitress arrived. After some prodding from Ryan, she'd decided to order a meal instead of an appetizer. Yet again he'd gotten his way. He'd reminded her of where they were, and she couldn't resist placing an order for one of her favorite dishes.

She chose the salmon with *beurre blanc* and roasted vegetables, while Ryan opted for a meal of steak medallions with potatoes and *haricot verts*.

To start, they each ordered a cup of the French onion soup.

The waitress tried to tempt them with wine, but knowing she'd need to keep a clear head, Shawna declined. She requested water with lemon and Ryan selected a bottle of Orangina soda.

She fiddled with the napkin on her lap before curiosity overwhelmed her. "How do you know my brother-in-law and sister?"

"I met William first," he said. "He and I go to the same bar, and one day we struck up a conversation and became friends. We happened to meet up there around the same time every so often to watch sports when he wasn't working late at the hospital. He likes to show off photos of his family. It's obvious how much he loves Yvonne and the kids.

"The last time I saw him, he mentioned his sweet and beautiful sister-in-law, and how he couldn't figure out why you weren't married. He hadn't talked about you much before then, and when he said your name, I couldn't believe it. I asked him your last name, and the next thing I know, he's showing me a picture of you."

"How did you convince him to set this up?"

"It wasn't easy. At first he said no way, but then he said he'd discuss it with Yvonne. She eventually came on board when I told her I'd been looking for you and how happy I was to find you again."

"My sister's smarter than that. She can usually see through BS."

"Maybe there wasn't any BS. I really am happy to find you."

His intense stare made Shawna uncomfortable. She played with the knife and fork on the table, moving them around before shifting them right back into the same position again.

"How long have you lived in Atlanta?" she asked.

"I moved here a few years ago. I'm a member of a few woodworking and custom furniture organizations. Someone in one of my networks heard about an owner selling his woodworking shop on the west end. It included the shop, the warehouse, and all the tools and machinery. After living in Oklahoma all my life, I wanted to leave and experience something different. I came to inspect the place and liked what I saw. The location was right, and the workers were anxious to please because they didn't want to lose their jobs. I had a CPA inspect the books, and after the seller turned over his list of clients to me, I bought the place."

"So you really did stay in custom furniture?"

Ryan nodded. "I was never cut out to sit in an office behind a desk. I need a scraper in my hand and the buzz of a power saw or sander in my head. The noise from the machines and the dust are like heaven to me. Few things are as enjoyable as building something from scratch. To consult with a client and take a product from a concept and create a useable piece of furniture—well, there's nothing else like it. Of course being in this kind of business wreaks havoc on your hands." He looked down at his palms.

His hands had been lightly calloused in Chicago from working on a farm most of his life and then as a woodworking apprentice. She'd never minded it, though.

"Congratulations on your success," Shawna said.

"Congratulations are in order for you, too. William told me you opened a boutique."

When she'd met Ryan, she'd finished school and worked at Saks Fifth Avenue, as she had every summer since her freshman year except when she went to France.

It had been her last summer with the company and they'd wanted to hire her on permanently, but she'd had other plans. She learned everything she could from them, the entire time thinking about her dream of one day opening her own store.

Nursing a wounded heart but determined to succeed, she'd opened a boutique named La Petite Robe a little over a year after moving to Atlanta. She chose Buckhead as the location, a major commercial district in the city. The astronomical lease initially caused her concern, but she'd made the right decision because the location turned out to be perfect, bringing in the type of clientele she longed to work with and who appreciated the designer clothing from New York and Paris.

Her success had surprised even her, but she probably wouldn't have accomplished what she had so quickly if it weren't for what had happened between her and Ryan. She'd put all her time and energy into the store, working hard to forget him and his lies, slicing in half her timetable to open the boutique.

The waitress arrived with the drinks and the soups.

"Thank you," Shawna said, about to dig in when she felt Ryan's gaze on her and saw the longing in his eyes. Her insides twisted painfully.

"Do you remember our first night together?" he asked.

She moistened her lips with her tongue but regretted it when he zeroed in on her mouth. Taking in a slow, deep breath, she wiped her damp palms on the napkin in her lap. "Are you going to keep doing that?"

"Doing what?"

"Make references to our night together."

"I thought that's why we were here."

"You're mistaken. We're here to catch up, not talk about the past."

"I don't think we can have one without the other."

"You're mistaken again."

He fell quiet and his silent observation caused a curious sensation to settle in her stomach. Ryan made her feel on edge and she had a sudden urge to scoot her chair back. The square table between them no longer seemed adequate.

"Are you telling me you don't think about it?" he asked quietly. "What it was like that first night?"

She'd thought about it often and had unfairly compared all her first dates and every other man to him over the years. They invariably fell short. Hard to believe how one night changed her life so much.

She shrugged, pretending a nonchalance she

was far from feeling. "Every now and again."

He leaned forward. "Liar."

Heat burned her cheeks, and she was grateful for her dark complexion so he couldn't see her embarrassment. "What do you want me to say?"

"I want you to admit that you think about it often, because I do. I have yet to meet a woman who measures up to you. The memory is as vivid as if it had been yesterday. I remember taking you out to dinner and you wore that bluish colored dress from work."

Teal, she corrected in her head. She remembered what he wore, too. He'd dressed up to impress her.

"I remember the look on your face when I pulled up in front of the restaurant."

"It was a nice restaurant. And a very expensive one, too."

His unwavering gaze held hers. "You were worth every dime. And more."

Chapter Five

Chicago, Friday, six years ago

Shawna couldn't hide her surprise when Ryan returned to Saks dressed in a white shirt, tie, and pressed slacks. He'd shaved off the day-old facial hair, and she smelled a hint of musk from his aftershave.

Her brows lifted. "You clean up well."

"I didn't make a good first impression so I figured I'd better bring my A-game. I passed this time?" Arms outstretched, he turned in a slow circle.

He definitely had a nice body and she whistled, noting the firm butt and narrow waist. "Not bad, Mr. Stewart."

"Which reminds me. You owe me something."

"What's that?"

"A last name."

"It's Ferguson."

"Shawna Ferguson," he said, as if committing it to memory.

"By the way, my co-workers have your name and they're writing down your license plate number as we speak. So don't do anything crazy."

"I wouldn't dream of doing anything crazy—unless you want me to." He drew a laugh when he wagged his eyebrows, and then he looked at the store to see two women standing at the window. He waved and they waved back. Returning his gaze to Shawna, he crooked his arm. "Your chariot awaits."

She looped her arm through his and followed to the illegally parked Lexus at the curb. She was enjoying this way too much even though she hardly knew him.

"Nice chariot."

"It's my brother's and so are the clothes."

"Maybe I should be going to dinner with your brother."

"Watch your mouth."

She laughed at the mock hurt expression on his face and slid onto the soft leather of the passenger seat. Ryan got in and took the wheel. She had no idea where they were headed, but she had a feeling that if he'd gone to this much trouble, she wouldn't be disappointed in his choice of restaurant.

Michigan Avenue, aka the Magnificent Mile, had no shortage of places to dine. Every type of cuisine could be found on the main road or down the side streets. When he pulled up in front of a turn-of-the-century brownstone, she almost gasped.

She'd eaten at the award-winning restaurant once and had fallen in love with the chef's ability to create flavorful dishes from seasonal choices. The *prix-fixe* menu only offered four- or five-course meal options and it wasn't cheap.

Shawna swung her gaze to Ryan.

He grinned, as if he knew he'd done good. "Still making a good impression?"

"Definitely."

Inside, large floral arrangements bursting with summer flowers adorned the dining room. Knock-offs of impressionist paintings and abstracts from local artists hung on the walls. A hostess escorted them to a table where they immediately ordered a four-course meal and a bottle of wine.

The time passed quickly, thanks to Ryan's sense of humor. By the time the cheese course arrived—a plated assortment of mild to sharp cheeses, accompanied by a baguette, sliced figs, dried apricots, and nuts—Shawna found herself laughing at everything he said. She didn't know if it was because he was so funny or because of the almost empty bottle on the table between them.

She rested her chin in one hand and swirled a glass of white wine in the other. "Okay, truth time. You're not unattractive so I can't figure out why you feel the need to follow women around and try to seduce them with expensive meals at French restaurants."

She sipped from the glass, eyeing him through her lashes over the rim. Oh boy, she was full-on flirting now. Maybe she needed to slow down. She set the glass on the table.

Leaning back in the chair, Ryan watched her with an amused expression. He tended to smile a lot, which was nice. It made his blue eyes sparkle like the sun bouncing off ocean waves.

"Is it working?"

"Yes, but you can't seriously tell me you don't have a girlfriend somewhere."

His smile wobbled before slipping back into place. "I don't."

For the first time since she'd sat down to dinner, she wondered if he had someone in his life, and the thought disturbed her enough that she lowered her gaze to the cheese plate and picked up a couple of walnuts. During that millisecond of time, envy filled her and the desire to make him hers overcame her.

Brushing aside the disquieting thoughts, Shawna continued the light-hearted banter they'd engaged in since the beginning of the meal. "Likes and dislikes," she said. "I love watching action movies, but none of my girlfriends like them, and I always end up going to the movies alone."

"Where have you been all my life?" Ryan folded his arms on the table and leaned forward, flexing his biceps oh so nicely. "Every woman I've ever dated hates action flicks. In the summer, I buy a movie package so I can see all the blockbusters at a discounted rate."

"Me, too!"

He reached for a nut at the same time she did, and their fingers brushed. They both pulled back quickly, and the unexpected jolt to Shawna's system stunned her. She lowered her eyes from

Ryan's gaze and inhaled to slow the rate of her beating heart. What had just happened?

Scraping his hand through his hair, Ryan cleared his throat. He couldn't ever remember being this nervous around a woman before. The simple act of brushing their fingertips against each other almost made him leap out of the chair.

"So, um . . . tell me about your trip to France." She'd mentioned earlier that she'd traveled to France while in college.

A wistful expression came over her features as she reflected on the fond memories. "I spent an amazing summer there after my freshman year." She had a nice voice. Low but feminine. He'd been asking her questions all night to hear her talk.

"I went only a few years ago but it seems much longer." She laughed. "I'd love to go back."

"You have to say something in French so I can hear you."

"Oh no, I couldn't." She looked embarrassed. If it wasn't for her russet complexion, he knew he'd see her cheeks redden.

"Why not? Maybe you can't really speak it fluently . . . ?" He let the question sit out there as a challenge, and right away she took the bait.

"Je parle français couramment, mais je préfère parler anglais parce que c'est ma langue maternelle."

His attraction to her catapulted into the stratosphere when she uttered the words. He definitely liked a French-speaking Shawna. Her voice had taken on a musical quality, as if she'd shifted into character when she spoke the language. Even though he had no idea what she'd said, the words happened to be some of the hottest he'd ever heard. The sudden movement against the zipper of his jeans proved how much he enjoyed them.

"What did you say?" he asked.

"I said I speak French fluently, but I prefer to speak in English because it's my native tongue."

Her smile blew him away. She had his undivided attention, and all of a sudden the thoughts that had plagued him since coming to visit his brother melted away. He ignored the guilt because all that mattered was right here, right now, with Shawna.

He was certain, in a way he hadn't been before, that she was the kind of woman—no, *the* woman—he wanted to be with. But she'd be leaving the day after tomorrow, moving back to South Carolina. The thought sobered him.

"What do you want to do tonight?" A loaded question. One that, if he answered it honestly himself, would involve them spending the night in the most intimate of ways. "Let's go to a movie," he offered.

"I'm not really in the mood for a movie." She twirled the stem of her glass on the table. "Ryan," she said thoughtfully, looking down into the Chardonnay. "I can't tell you how much—"

"How about dancing?" he rushed out. "You said you like to dance." He didn't want the night to end.

"I do."

"There's got to be somewhere we can go. What do you usually do on a Friday night?"

"Sometimes I go out." She paused, giving him

a considering look. "There's a place not too far from here. My co-workers and I have gone a few times. It's in the basement of a building and has this whole house-party vibe. They play a lot of songs from the eighties and nineties."

"Sounds like fun."

"Ryan, I leave in a couple of days."

"All the more reason to pack in as much as we can tonight, right?" He reached across the table and took one of her hands in both of his. The same jolt of electricity vibrated through his fingers, but this time he didn't pull away. This time he embraced it, enclosing her smaller hand and holding on tighter when her fingers trembled. "I just want to spend time with you. I feel like something's happening here, and I don't . . . I-I . . ."

He fumbled, searching for the right words and coming up short, unable to explain what was happening but knowing he didn't want to get off this ride they were on.

But maybe he hadn't totally screwed up. Because she smiled the sweetest, softest smile that turned his insides to mush.

"I know what you mean," she said softly.

Chapter Six

After circling the area several times, Ryan parked the car a few blocks from the venue. They took a set of stone steps below street level where music poured from the open doorway of a townhouse basement.

A few men loitered outside, smoking cigarettes and watching the women walk in wearing their booty-hugging dresses and sky-high heels. The predominantly African-American crowd squeezed into a space too small to accommodate a group of that size, resulting in a fire marshal's wet dream.

Stuffed into a corner on a makeshift stage, the deejay called out, "Did y'all come here to paaaartay?"

A resounding, "Yeah!" erupted from the dancers.

"This place is crazy," Ryan said. His breath tickled her ear.

She nodded in agreement. "It's always like this."

They stood on the edge of the crowd, watching everyone shake and shimmy.

"Do you want to dance?" he asked.

As much as Shawna wanted to, she hesitated. How much rhythm did he have? "Why don't we stand back and watch for a minute?"

He nodded. "That's probably best. I'm not much of a dancer." After a few minutes, he dipped his head to her ear again. "If you want to dance, go ahead. I'll stand here and watch."

"You came here to watch?"

He placed a hand at her lower back, and the touch sent sparks dancing along the base of her spine. "I like to watch." His steady gaze held hers, leaving no doubt as to what he'd implied by the words. He straightened, his attention drawn back to the dancers.

Shawna rubbed the goose bumps from her arms.

"I'm going to get something to drink. You want anything?" he asked. She shook her head. "Be right back."

She watched him disappear to the other end of the room in the direction of a small bar.

"Hey, you want to dance?" A black guy with dreads stood beside her.

She looked over at Ryan, now engrossed in conversation with the bartender. He *had* given her permission to dance.

"Sure," she said with a shrug.

She and Dreadlocks squeezed between the bodies and started dancing, but after several songs, Shawna broke away from him when he got too handsy.

She looked around for Ryan. As the only white male in a sea of black faces, he shouldn't be hard to find, but she didn't see him anywhere.

Outside she asked a couple of people if they'd seen him. No one had. She climbed the steps up to the street and looked around but didn't see any sign of him. She wondered if she'd offended him by dancing with another guy. But she couldn't have, because he'd given her permission to. Hadn't he?

She went back inside to search for him, and that's when she saw him.

Shawna couldn't believe her eyes. Her mouth fell open. Ryan was dancing, shaking his hips and bouncing his shoulders to LL Cool J's "Jingling Baby." His dance partner practically did a strip tease in front of him, tossing her long tresses and working her voluptuous body in a series of provocative gyrations.

The next thing Shawna knew, another woman danced up behind him and created a Ryan sandwich. He handled them both by switching back and forth, turning every so often to give each woman his attention, and even incorporated spanking motions with his hands.

Someone nudged her in the arm. "You better go get your man." The warning was issued, and then the woman walked away.

As the song flowed into another, Shawna made her way over to Ryan.

"Hey." He smiled but kept on dancing.

"I couldn't find you. Where were you?" She yelled to be heard over the music.

"In the bathroom for a sec."

"I'm ready to dance now." She gave the women dirty looks.

Ryan stopped and smiled apologetically to both of them. When they walked away, Shawna narrowed her eyes at him.

"You played me."

He flashed his teeth. "No. You played yourself."

Chubb Rock's "Treat 'Em Right" started his shoulders bouncing and feet moving again, and Shawna shook her head and started moving, too. She would have to watch him.

****

The night air wafted across Shawna's face and cooled her heated body. "I had so much fun!"

The venue had shut down and the partiers disbursed, heading for their cars. Her feet hurt after being in heels all day and spending the last few hours dancing, but she didn't regret it.

"Should I be offended that you sound so surprised?" Ryan had removed his tie and stuck it into the right pocket of his pants. He looked more relaxed with one button undone at the top of his shirt.

"No. What do you mean?"

"Didn't think the white guy could dance, huh?"

Embarrassed, she slanted a sheepish grin at him. "There's not an anti-defamation league I have to answer to, is there?"

He laughed, the sound especially attractive as they walked along the dark street. "Not this time. I'm giving you a pass."

"Thank you."

Up ahead, a man with a handwritten cardboard sign on a food cart offered sausage dogs for sale. "Do you mind if I stop and get a bite to eat?" Ryan asked as they neared.

"Are you sure you want to do that? He's always out here after the parties selling his overpriced hotdogs."

"Right now, I'd mortgage my parents' farm for a bite."

"How is that possible? We didn't eat that long ago."

"We sat for a long time talking in the restaurant, and we ate almost eight hours ago," Ryan pointed out. "Do you want anything?"

"No, you go ahead."

They waited in line while the vendor served others. When Ryan's turn came, he ordered a spicy sausage dog with everything and purchased a bottle of water. They started walking again, and he lifted the napkin-wrapped hotdog, taking a third into his mouth with a big bite.

"Mmm. This is good." He spoke around a mouthful of meat and bread. "Sure you don't want some?"

Shawna looked at the sandwich. The alluring smell of onions, sauerkraut, and relish moistened her taste buds. "You don't have cooties, do you?"

"No, I was immunized from them years ago."

She grinned. She felt relaxed with him, as if she'd known him forever. "In that case . . ."

They stopped a few feet from the car and he held out the hotdog. As she opened her mouth, their gazes met. She became very aware that she was taking a bite from the exact same spot where his mouth had been. All of a sudden, the act seemed very intimate. The smile on Ryan's face eased away as if the same thought crossed his mind at the same moment. His eyes went from being filled with humor to darkening with something that looked very much like lust.

Shawna's chest tightened and she diverted her gaze to the hotdog, sinking her teeth into it and quickly withdrawing when she'd pulled off a small chunk.

"Good?"

She nodded, still unable to look at him. He offered his water and she hesitated this time. A quick look showed him watching her closely. She took the bottle and their fingertips grazed each other, sending pleasurable warmth throughout her chest.

After taking a mouthful, she handed back the bottle. "Thank you."

They stood in silence for a moment before Ryan erased the small distance between them with one step. "Shawna—"

"I'm ready to go to the hotel now." She started feeling things she didn't want to feel, hadn't expected to feel when she came out tonight. A temptation that unsettled her and made her suddenly ill at ease. Ryan should have been a temporary diversion, but right now she felt he could be much more than that.

Among her friends, she was the good one, the one who always did everything right. She'd never had a one-night stand—only long-term relationships. When she and her friends went out, it went without saying that she'd be the designated driver. But the more time she spent with Ryan, the less she wanted to be good.

But her priorities were to finish her summer job and open her own boutique. A man didn't figure into the picture until later on down the road. Certainly not one she'd never see again come the day after tomorrow.

Ryan finished his hotdog and got into the car, and before long they were on their way. Shawna huddled close to the door, sitting as far away from him as she could, which didn't seem far enough. The mood of the evening had changed. No more light-hearted banter or teasing smiles. A veil of tension settled over them, hindering the ability to speak.

On the road to the hotel, the weighted air wouldn't go away. Ryan fiddled with the tuner on the radio and finally settled on a station playing music. At that time of night, slow jams filled the airwaves, and a woman sang an invitation to a distant lover in a sultry voice that served to stretch Shawna's nerves even tauter.

When they arrived at The Haven Hotel, Ryan pulled into the underground parking garage instead of dropping her at the front.

"What are you doing?"

"I'm going to escort you to your room."

"You'll have to pay for parking."

"It's not that much and it'll be worth it." He shut off the engine. "Let's go."

Her hands shook as she reached for the door.

The tension between them magnified in the quiet elevator, and so did the heaviness that had settled in her stomach. By the time they reached her room, she was a nervous wreck with sweaty palms and wobbly knees.

She fumbled with the key card before finally fitting the plastic strip into the narrow slot and hearing the door click open.

"Shawna?" Ryan said, so close behind her that his lips brushed her earlobe, affecting every nerve from the top of her head to the tips of her toes.

"Yes?" The word came out in a breathless whisper.

"I'm coming in."

She almost sagged with relief. Her eyes found his over her shoulder, and without a word, she led the way inside.

Chapter Seven

Present day, Atlanta

Shawna managed to enjoy the meal, despite the company she shared it with. She'd never had a bad meal here, and every bite had been as delicious as expected.

She'd never had a bad experience here either—until this evening. Now every time she came back to this restaurant, she'd remember tonight's awkwardness. How seeing Ryan had caused her to recall moments in her past that she'd never truly forgotten but that she'd managed to suppress for a long time.

"Why did you follow me that day? If you'd let me go, we would've never seen each other again."

Across the table, Ryan watched her closely. "I know. That's why I followed you."

His words wreaked havoc with her emotions. She took a sip of water. "What were your expectations for tonight?"

She knew he couldn't read her mind and know what she'd been thinking, but his scrutiny still made her uncomfortable. "I didn't have any. I wanted to see you, that's all."

"Why?"

He paused, mulling the question before answering. "I never got the chance to apologize that last day in Chicago. What happened stayed with me for a long time afterward. *You* stayed with me for a long time afterward. For months after I left Chicago, I would wake up in the middle of the night at random times, thinking about you. Wondering what you were doing and who you were with. Did you find someone to make you happy. Someone you could trust and believe in, who wasn't me."

Sadly, in the past six years, no other man had come close to making her feel the way he did, but she'd never admit it to him.

"When William showed you the photo, you could have pretended not to know me. Chances are we would have never met."

"Impossible. Besides, I don't think you're sorry to see me. I think you're surprised, but once the shock wears off, you won't be so upset."

Shawna crossed her arms over her chest. "Just like that, you think everything will be fine because you want it to be?"

"That's not what I said."

"It's what you meant." She shook her head. "You're still selfish, Ryan, only caring about what's best for you. You felt guilty about what happened so, to ease your conscience, you set up a phony date and now you're trying to convince me to not only forgive you, but not be upset. Let's pretend you never hurt and humiliated me, and then what? Maybe we hook up again?"

His mouth tightened. "Do you want me to deny that I thought about it? I won't, because you're right. Something happened between us in Chicago, and I admit that a part of me wondered if we could recapture what we had."

"We didn't have anything in Chicago because it was wrong," Shawna said coldly.

"It wasn't wrong!" Ryan spoke with such vehemence it startled her. He swiped a hand across his mouth and took a calming breath. "It was us. The timing may have been off, but *we* weren't wrong. We were right."

How could he say that? He actually sat there rewriting history.

"How's Holly?" Shawna asked.

He stiffened. "I don't want to talk about her."

"Why not? Because you can't face the fact that you lied to me?"

"I wanted to tell you the truth, Shawna."

"Wanted, but didn't. You should have told me the truth before we slept together. Can you deny that the only reason I slept with you is because you betrayed her and deceived me?"

He looked at her with deadpan eyes. At least he didn't avoid her gaze like he had that day. He didn't acknowledge her words, but he didn't refute them either. How could he, when it was true?

"Isn't that what you call it," she continued, "when you're sleeping with one woman while involved with another?"

Chapter Eight

Chicago, Saturday, six years ago

Sunlight teased Shawna's eyelids open. The hotel room's thick drapes were wide apart, allowing the rays to enter. She could see Saks Fifth Avenue across the street. She'd explained to Ryan that she'd done the store a favor by staying on a few extra days, but yesterday had been her last day. With her lease up at her apartment and a new tenant moving in right away, Saks had moved her into this hotel at the company's expense, making it a nice way to end the summer.

She stretched and yawned, lazily brushing hair from her face. Behind her, Ryan mumbled grumpily about it being too early to be up. She refrained from pointing out it wasn't early. They were late.

A heavy arm fell across her waist under the fluffy white duvet. He kissed a spot between her shoulder blades, and the rough hairs of a reemerging beard scraped her skin. He reached up to fondle her breasts, his fingers stroking a circle around a hardened nipple.

"Are you up?" he whispered. He obviously knew that she was or he was a very inconsiderate person. He tweaked the hard peak of her breast and pressed his body against hers.

"Mmm." Shawna reached back and touched the morning wood wedged between them. "So are you."

A puff of air ruffled the hair at the back of her neck when he laughed and slid his muscular thigh between hers.

They'd made love twice last night. The first time had been slow and sweet as they took their time exploring each other's bodies. He was such an attentive lover, leaving not one square inch of skin untouched. Because of him she learned that the backs of her knees were erogenous zones. She bit her lip at the memory of his kisses there, smiling to herself.

The second time had been more passionate because of their newfound familiarity.

"Last night was nice," Shawna said softly.

"Nice?" He sounded offended.

"Excellent," she corrected.

"That's better."

She wiggled back into him. She'd only had a couple of lovers since she lost her virginity in college, but neither of them had ever made her feel like this. Content in a way she'd never been before. How was it possible to feel so comfortable with someone she'd known less than twenty-four hours?

Despite being a bundle of nerves, upon arrival to the room she'd known that she wanted to spend the night with him. Straight-laced Shawna, voted Best Personality and Most Likely to Succeed by her class, had had a one-night stand and it didn't feel wrong like she would've thought. It felt right. Perfect. Because he was perfect.

He made her feel sexy. Last night she'd insisted on taking a shower when they came in. After working all day and dancing half the night, she'd wanted to freshen up. In the bathroom, she'd rubbed scented lotion all over her skin.

A shirtless Ryan had reclined on the bed watching music videos. When she exited the bathroom in her black and white La Perla bra and matching panties, his mouth had fallen open and his breathing had kicked up a notch. The scalloped edges of the bra barely contained her breasts, pushing them together so they very nearly spilled from confinement. She'd almost burst into giggles at the expression on his face. She knew then that she'd more than lived up to his expectations.

"Wow."

"You like?"

"I like." His Adam's apple had bobbed as he swallowed. He kept looking at her with an intensity in his eyes that simultaneously flattered and made her anxious. His gaze had skimmed over her breasts, her bare belly, and her hips. "I like so much I might be forced to tear those pretty panties off of you."

"Not these. They're La Perla. Very expensive."

"Then you shouldn't have put them on."

She'd thought at first he was kidding, but he hadn't been. The lines in his face had sharpened, and his breathing had become labored. His obvious excitement had fueled her own.

She thought about how much he made her laugh, too. His sense of humor had worn through her flimsy reservations last night, and she'd done something she never would've expected. She'd had no well-formulated plan with step-by-step instructions to consult. For the first time in her life, she'd lived in the moment and colored outside the lines. It had been scary but exhilarating.

"I think I'm a breast man," Ryan said now. His hand had remained on her breast the entire time, and he squeezed the soft flesh, eliciting a moan from Shawna.

"I think you're a butt man," she said, pushing back, aching for him.

"Yeah, that too. And I'm an arm man." He nipped a spot below her shoulder. She pushed back against him again and he started a slow grind that made her wet. "We have to stop. I don't have any more condoms." But he kept grinding and she kept rubbing.

"Okay," Shawna said in a breathless voice. "In a minute. Let me . . ." Her voice trailed off as she arched her back.

He applied more pressure to her breasts, caressing them both, his calloused hand wreaking havoc on the sensitive nipples.

"Are you trying to come?" Ryan asked against the spot behind her ear. His voice sounded strained.

"Mhmm."

He applied pressure to her sensitive core by lifting his thigh higher between her legs. Shawna gasped and closed her eyes, sinking her teeth into her lower lip as she concentrated. Her body's juices coated his leg as she worked her hips with gusto, and Ryan continued to squeeze her breasts, using both hands now. He filled his palms with the luscious mounds, groaning into her hair.

They worked themselves into a frenzy. Grunting and moaning, panting heavily, they continued their gyrations in the throes of arousal.

"Does that feel good, love?" he whispered.

"Yes! Oh, Ryan, right there. Please. Yes . . . *right there.*"

Her desperate pleas riled him up, and he pumped his leg at the apex of her thighs. He pinched her nipples and she cried out, shattering in his arms. The sound of her feminine cries made heat crawl across his skin.

With one swift movement, he had her flipped onto her stomach. Gripping her hips, he buried his face in her hair and began to furiously hump against her soft bottom. If he couldn't get inside her, he'd do the next best thing to relieve the pressure in his groin.

He stiffened. Fingers closed around his erection, he released into his hands, surrendering to the crushing climax that gripped him. Some of his come dripped onto her back. Cursing, he mumbled an apology and fell onto the bed, his breathing labored.

He watched Shawna slip from the bed and rush to the bathroom. She came back with a warm damp washcloth. He cleaned himself off and then looked over at her. A beaming smile lit up her eyes. Damn, she was beautiful. Not just her face. She had inner beauty, and it made her more attractive on the outside.

"You made quite a mess," she said.

"It's your fault." With a gentle tackle, he rolled her onto her back, and she giggled, wrapping her arms around his neck. "You know what the first thing on my to-do list is today?" he asked.

"What?"

"Buy condoms."

****

They ordered breakfast from room service. Ryan dragged a table to the window and they ate in front of it, wrapped in the hotel's white robes. While eating, they talked constantly. He found out that she'd acquired skills in visual merchandising and retail management that she planned to apply when she opened her own boutique one day.

She learned he had business aspirations, too. Bored, he'd dropped out of college and told his parents he wanted to make custom furniture. He'd always enjoyed earning extra money when he worked with his carpenter uncle. Later, he'd discovered that his true passion lay in building furniture.

At first his decision alarmed his parents. They'd wanted him to pursue a professional career, the same as his older brother, a successful attorney in Chicago.

Ryan knew he'd never be like his brother, and he'd been worried about disappointing his father and mother. They hadn't been pleased with his decision and had sat him down for a serious conversation about the pros and cons of his plans.

Eventually, they'd accepted his choice, even if they didn't approve. His father encouraged him to apprentice under a professional, which he'd been doing for the past few years. He'd already earned a reputation for quality work and filled side orders for a few customers.

In the midst of their conversation, Ryan's phone rang. Shawna watched him leap up from the table and pull it from his pants on the floor. He stared down at the screen, and instead of answering it, he turned it off and stuck it back in his pocket.

"Why didn't you answer it?" she asked.

He came back to the table and plopped into the chair across from her. "It was my brother." He didn't look at her; instead, he stabbed a piece of fruit with his fork.

"You should've talked to him," Shawna said lightly. She watched closely, sensing a change in him. "He's probably worried because you've been out all night in his clothes and his car."

"He knows I'm a big boy and can take care of myself. I'll call him later." Popping a strawberry in his mouth, he finally looked at her and grinned.

The smile didn't quite make it to his eyes this time.

He was lying.

Chapter Nine

Chicago, Sunday, six years ago

After taking a quick shower, Ryan dressed hurriedly in the bathroom. He'd only come back to change clothes and drop off his brother's car. The past two days with Shawna had been the best days he could ever remember. At his request, she agreed to stay an extra day and fly back to South Carolina tomorrow.

He needed time to think because he hadn't been able to get much thinking done while in her presence. He'd been so focused on her and how she made him feel.

When he'd told his brother about his feelings for her, he'd asked Ryan if he'd lost his mind. "You have to stop being so impulsive, Ryan. It's exciting now, but how long will that last? You don't even know her. Have your fun, but don't throw away a solid relationship for some girl you met the other day."

Ryan knew he simply didn't understand. Shawna wasn't *some girl*. He'd fallen for her.

As ridiculous as it sounded, he knew it was true. They'd only known each other a short time, but how else to explain this urgent need to get back to her? How else to explain the rush of excitement at the thought of laying eyes on her or the crush of pain he felt in his chest when he thought about her flying out of his life tomorrow?

He stared at his reflection. If he felt so strongly about her, he had to tell the truth, because no good could come from starting a relationship based on a lie. Today at brunch, he resolved, he'd tell her the truth and hope that she understood.

As he shoved his foot into the second tennis shoe, the doorbell rang. Quickly, he tied the shoelace and raced to the door. Peering out the peephole, his heart plummeted when he saw an unexpected face.

What the . . . ?

Ryan ran his fingers through his hair, his mind racing.

The doorbell rang again, longer this time. Taking a deep breath, he opened the door.

"Surprise!" The perky blonde dropped her bag and flung her arms around his neck.

Ryan returned a tepid hug. "Holly, what are you doing here?"

"Is that any way to greet your girlfriend?" She pouted up at him.

Holly Cullen, the reason he took the trip to Chicago. He'd needed to get away from the constant pressure of marriage talk. It seemed everyone knew he and Holly should get married—their friends and family, Holly, her parents, his parents. Everyone except Ryan.

He'd known her forever. They'd gone to the same schools, and their parents were best friends, so their families spent time together often. Once old enough to date, it was understood they would date each other, which they did, but broke up for a while when they went to college. They both moved back home after she graduated and he dropped out, and they'd been dating off and on ever since.

Eventually, Holly started hinting around about marriage, and his mother and hers added pressure. In his head it made perfect sense that marriage should be the next step in their relationship, but his heart wasn't in it.

He cared about Holly a lot, and he thought she'd make a good wife. She knew how to cook, worked at a daycare center, and was great with kids. But the more he thought about getting married to her, the more it felt like what others expected him to do. Not what *he* wanted to do.

"I didn't know you were coming," Ryan said, bringing her bag into the living room.

"That's because I wanted to surprise you, silly. Wow, this is nice." Her mouth hung open as she walked deeper into the apartment. Ryan and his brother had different tastes. Where Ryan would have gone for a more rustic abode, his brother's home impressed with sleek lines and modern technology. A remote controlled everything, from the lights to the appliances.

"It is a great place," Ryan agreed. The almost two weeks he'd spent there had been pleasant, but now his refuge had been disrupted by the person he'd been seeking escape from.

"It's gorgeous." Holly flung open the drapes and looked down at the street.

Ryan glanced at his watch. He had to meet Shawna for brunch in a few minutes. "Um, Holly, what are you doing here?"

"I came to see you, Ryan. You haven't been returning my calls."

"I've been busy. How did you get here?"

"I flew."

No way she'd bought a ticket on the spur of the moment to come out and see him. It would've been cost-prohibitive, so she must have bought the ticket long before and been planning this all along.

"I told you I wanted to come out here to think." He tried to keep the frustration out of his voice, but he heard it creeping in.

"About what? Are you reconsidering your career in making furniture?" She asked the question with a hopeful tone in her voice. "Not that there's anything wrong with that," she added hastily.

Sometimes he wondered if she really loved him, or did she love the thought of getting married. Or, did she simply go along with everyone else's expectations.

Her idea of the perfect spouse meant a professional man with a degree who wore dress shirts and ties and went into the office every day. She'd bragged about him when he studied information systems, but when she found out he'd left college, she hadn't been pleased. She hadn't understood his passion for his work, and for a few days they hadn't spoken after he told her. Then out of the blue, she called and said she could work with it.

By contrast, Shawna hadn't batted an eye when he told her about his career choice. She hadn't judged him for being a college dropout. In fact, she'd been curious about his work and asked him questions about the types of machinery he used and the process involved from the blueprint to the finished product.

"I'm not rethinking my career. I came out here to think about my life and my future, and I wanted to do that without any distractions."

Her brow wrinkled with concern and she pouted. "Your life and your future are *our* life and *our* future. I can help. Aren't you happy to see me?"

A perfect example of why he needed to get away. She suffocated him, and he felt cornered by her desire for marriage.

Now he felt like a pile of horse dung. Holly had a way of manipulating him with guilt. He knew she did it, yet he allowed it to happen. "Of course I am," he lied. "I've been thinking about you." Though not in the way she thought.

"Good," she said with a sigh. "For a minute, I thought you didn't want to see me." She laughed as if the very idea was ridiculous.

Now would be the time to broach the topic of their relationship, but he chickened out. She'd come all this way to see him, and he didn't have the guts to tell her that he'd met someone. And what about his brother's advice? *Was* he throwing away his future?

"I've been worried about you, Pooky Wooky." She walked over and circled her arms around his neck, while at the same time Ryan tried not to wince at the pet name. When his friends had found out about it, they'd ragged him mercilessly for months.

His mind shifted gears to Shawna. Sexy, curvy Shawna. It had been hard as hell to leave her this morning, but the promise to meet up again sustained him. He couldn't wait to climb into bed with her one more time and run his tongue along the curve of her hip, suck those dark brown nipples—which he'd come to think of as his own—into his mouth to savor and enjoy while she gasped with pleasure.

"Ooh, you do miss me, don't you?" Holly reached down and covered his hard-on.

He laughed uneasily and pulled his pelvis away from her. "Whoa, let's slow down for a minute. I don't have any condoms, so we can't do anything." A boldfaced lie because he'd bought a new pack. He hadn't used them all, but he'd put in a good effort to get rid of as many as he could with Shawna. "Are you hungry? I was about to go eat."

Holly's mouth puckered into another pout. She rubbed his chest. "I'd rather stay here with you, but I can't let my man starve. Let's go put food in your tummy. Then I'll be your dessert." She rose up on her toes and gave him a quick peck on the mouth.

Ryan swallowed down his discomfort and followed her out the door. He didn't know what to do yet, but he knew he had to think of something fast.

****

Shawna sat in the lobby of the hotel waiting for Ryan. Maybe she'd misunderstood the arrangement. Were they supposed to meet here and walk to brunch together, or was she supposed to meet him at his brother's apartment?

She tried calling him, but his phone rang several times before going to voice mail. She sent him a text and then went into the hotel restaurant to get something to eat. The menu items looked delicious, but she didn't have much of an appetite.

While a string quartet played soft music in the background, she sat in the lavishly decorated dining room, worried that she'd misread Ryan. They'd been getting along so well. Surely it hadn't all been pretense on his part.

She'd hoped they could stay in touch, that their romance wouldn't be reduced to a two-night tryst that didn't have a future. True, he lived in Oklahoma and she in South Carolina, but they could continue to see each other if they wanted to make it work.

She'd wait a little while longer. Maybe she'd simply misunderstood, or something had come up. He'd respond to one of her messages eventually.

****

Ryan thought he'd never get away from Holly. He left her at the elevator and hurried out of the apartment building.

While Holly had discussed menu options with

the waitress at the restaurant, he'd managed to send a quick text to Shawna and tell her he'd see her soon.

Now on his way, he didn't know what he'd say. The summer sun beat down on him, and he wasn't sure if that's what caused a sweat to break out on his forehead, or the predicament he'd gotten himself into.

He couldn't spend the night with Shawna with Holly in town. He couldn't spend the night with Holly when he'd asked Shawna to postpone her trip home so they could have more time together. He had to choose, and the person he didn't choose would be hurt. But which one?

He knew which one. The only real option meant telling Shawna the truth and hoping that she'd forgive him. Then he'd have to face Holly and the fallout from her disappointment that their relationship was over. He didn't want to hurt her, but he couldn't think of any way to spare her feelings.

Outside the building, he called Shawna.

"Ryan? What's going on? Did I get our plans mixed up?"

"No, you didn't. I'm sorry, love. I had a . . . situation I needed to take care of. Where are you right now?"

"I'm—" She stopped, and that's when he saw her.

They looked at each other from a short distance. Today she wore jeans, a white V-necked T-shirt that molded over her ample breasts, a wide belt, heels, and chunky jewelry. She always looked so put together.

"I came to see you," she said softly. She sounded unsure.

Ryan lowered the phone and started toward her, determined to allay her fears and soothe away any doubts she had about what she'd come to mean to him.

"Yoohoo, Ryan, there you are."

He stopped moving and held his breath.

That was Holly's voice behind him, and it resonated like a record scratch in the musical interlude of this perfect moment.

Chapter Ten

Shawna looked past him, curiosity etched in her features. Ryan couldn't even turn around. He kept hoping he'd collapsed after hitting his head in the shower back at his brother's apartment.

Wake up. Wake up!

Holly came to stand beside him and snaked her arm around his. "Who's this?"

The curiosity in Shawna's eyes turned to confusion and then segued into hurt. She blinked rapidly and took a deep breath in an obvious attempt to compose herself.

Holly tugged on his arm. "Pooky, you're being rude."

"I . . . ah . . . Holly, this is Shawna. Shawna, this is Holly." Here was his opportunity to come clean, and he couldn't. Not like this.

"Nice to meet you, Shawna. I'm Ryan's girlfriend."

"Girlfriend?" Shawna repeated.

"Yes. We've known each other all our lives, and we're practically engaged. I came to surprise him because I've missed him the past couple of weeks." She squeezed his arm, seemingly unaware of the damage she'd caused by her announcement.

Later, when he'd had time to think, he'd recognize what had happened. Holly had immediately seen the threat Shawna presented. She'd known and effectively claimed her rightful place in his life.

Right now, he couldn't see it because of his shell-shocked state. Right now, he didn't know if he was coming or going, and he could only think of finding a way to fix this. But how?

Holly continued. "Then I get here, and he tells me how much he's missed me and been thinking about me. I couldn't ask for a better guy." She looked up at Ryan, her gaze filled with adoration.

Shawna studied Ryan. Color smeared his cheeks and he couldn't even look her in the eye.

"Look at him. He's blushing," Holly said. "I've embarrassed him."

That wasn't embarrassment. That was guilt.

He and Holly looked good together, like an advertisement for a dating website. The pretty blonde held onto him as if she feared one of the city's strong winds would swoop down and lift him away.

All Shawna's ideas about seeing where this could go effectively extinguished. "You didn't mention you have a girlfriend."

"How do the two of you know each other?" Holly asked.

"I work at Saks Fifth Avenue, and he approached me and asked if I could help him find a gift for someone. I guess for you."

Ryan's stomach muscles clenched in dread. She could bust him right now. Why didn't she? Or did she plan to, and those statements were simply the lead up to the big reveal that he'd cheated on his girlfriend?

If she exposed his dishonesty to Holly, everyone back home would know what a jerk he was. That he'd come to Chicago and had a fling—cheating on the woman he'd practically been destined to marry.

He'd thought about giving up a future with her, a woman whom he knew well, their families knew each other, and all for what? For a woman he'd known only a couple of days.

But she made him feel more alive and excited about the prospect of being with someone than he'd ever felt. Forever with Shawna didn't cause the same sense of dread as forever with Holly.

"Well, he didn't give me a gift," Holly said, "so I guess he didn't get anything."

"Or he did get something, but he's keeping it a secret from you."

A tightening in the back of Ryan's throat kept him from speaking. He avoided Shawna's eyes, staring out at the bustling street filled with cars and pedestrians. Everyone on their way somewhere. He'd been on his way somewhere, too. To see Shawna and spend time with her.

Now he couldn't even look at her because of the guilt he felt and the hurt he'd caused. What could he say? He'd denied being involved with someone. He'd misled her.

"I'm glad I met you, Holly. Ryan, I'm glad we ran into each other and I had the opportunity to meet your girlfriend."

He stared down at the concrete. She sounded so cool, her voice so controlled, as if they really were mere acquaintances and hadn't been lovers. As if she hadn't become as essential to him as breathing. Meanwhile, for the past few minutes he'd been unable to speak, words deadlocked in his throat.

"Have a nice life."

The words sounded so final, he found the courage to look at her. She only offered a brief moment of eye contact. He saw the hurt and anger before she walked away, poised, hips swaying in her tight jeans.

"She seems nice," Holly said. "I thought that we could . . ."

Her voice droned on, but he didn't hear anything else she said. Shawna had walked away and he hadn't done anything to stop her. He had a flash of memory—of being buried inside of her hot, wet body. Of her head tipped back, silky dark hair spilled across the pillows as his tongue licked the sweat from her damp skin. Memories of her thighs clenched around his hips, and how he'd come so hard he almost blacked out.

He knew without a doubt his life would never be the same.

****

Ryan finally escaped after he told Holly he'd ordered a pizza for them to eat and had to go pick it up. More lies. He didn't know what to do in such a messy situation, but he knew he had to see Shawna.

In the brightly lit lobby of The Haven Hotel, he approached the front desk. He couldn't get upstairs without having a key card. He hadn't phoned Shawna because he suspected she wouldn't answer. He wouldn't blame her, but he hoped she'd give him a chance to explain.

He asked the person at the front desk to ring her room.

Seconds later, the woman frowned at the screen in front of her. "I'm sorry, sir, but Miss Ferguson has already checked out."

Alarm bubbled up inside of him. "That can't be right. She doesn't leave until tomorrow."

"No, Miss Ferguson—"

"Check again!"

The woman tensed and stared at him as if he'd pulled a gun on her. A guest checking in a few feet away looked over at him. A man who carried himself with the authority of a manager talked to another guest off to the side. He broke away from the conversation and came over.

"Is everything okay here? Can I help you?"

"I need her to check the system one more time. That's all," Ryan explained. Did he look as desperate as he felt? The hand he used to gesture toward the woman behind the desk shook slightly. He spoke slowly to curtail the panic from taking over his central nervous system. It was imperative that he maintain control before they dragged him out of there kicking and screaming like a lunatic. "She said Shawna Ferguson has checked out, but that can't be right. Sh-she's supposed to leave tomorrow, not today."

The manager nodded at the woman behind the counter, and she proceeded to review the system again. Her fingers tapped the keyboard. "It says here she checked out at six o'clock this evening." She looked up at him with pity in her eyes. "I'm sorry, sir. She's gone."

Chapter Eleven

"You never answered my question," Shawna said. "How is Holly nowadays?"

"I haven't seen her in a long time. We broke up."

"I'm sorry to hear that." Sorry for Holly mostly because she'd seemed to love Ryan.

"Don't be. It was for the best. She found the right man for her and got married. He's a dentist and they have two kids." The waitress came by to check on them, and when they told her they didn't need anything, she moved on to another table in her station. "How about you? Are you seeing anyone seriously?"

"My sister wouldn't have set us up if I had a boyfriend. Are *you* dating anyone seriously? Please answer honestly this time."

A rueful smile twisted the corner of his lips.

"No, I'm not because no one compares to you."

"Stop it. Stop making everything about me."

"Everything is about you."

"I said stop it, Ryan, or I'll leave." She wouldn't fall prey to his charms again. After what he'd done, she shouldn't even be seated at a table with him.

Silence extended between them, and in want of something to do, Shawna sipped her water. Her gaze arced over the rest of the diners. Some engaged in animated conversations. Others— mainly the pairs of people eating together— appeared more intimate. She easily discerned which ones were lovers. It was obvious in the little acts of affection, such as the man stroking the woman's hand on the table near them. Or the couple seated in the booth in the corner, sharing a dessert with the same fork.

By contrast, she and Ryan made it obvious they were not lovers. They sat across the table from each other and hadn't touched since they'd been seated. If she could move farther away from him, she would.

So different from how they'd been together before the reality of Holly intruded. Memories flooded her mind—memories of flirtatious laughter, play-fighting, and making love beneath white sheets until every muscle felt drained of energy because she'd been thoroughly satisfied.

Dragging her thoughts from the past, Shawna drained her glass of water and signaled a passing waiter for a refill. She needed to cool down from the titillating thoughts. She also needed to do a better job of regulating which paths her mind chose to wander down so she could maintain the wall of animosity necessary to remain unaffected by Ryan.

"I wish you hadn't left the hotel that evening," he said.

Her gaze swung back to him. "You mean after I saw you and your girlfriend? There was no reason for me to stick around. I certainly wouldn't allow you back into my bed, and I'm sure Holly wouldn't have approved of us spending any time together."

"Don't be too sure."

"What did you say?" Shawna asked sharply. She must have misheard.

"I told Holly about us once she and I went back to Oklahoma. She forgave me—said that she understood if I needed to get one last fling out of my system before we settled down." He laughed, an empty, hollow sound. A pained expression came over his face. "I wish things had been different. That you had been the one to forgive me and she'd been the one to walk away."

"Don't say that."

"It's true. I never stopped thinking about you. I tried to find you in South Carolina. I still thought about you, and I thought if I could get a chance to talk to you and explain, you'd understand."

She'd changed her number shortly after she left Chicago because her sister had decided to move to Atlanta with her new husband and Shawna had followed, seeking new opportunities.

"Understand what? You made me the other woman."

"That was never my intention."

"What *was* your intention, because I don't understand. Why approach me when you had a girlfriend?"

"I honestly don't know. I didn't think far enough ahead. I regret the way I handled things, but I couldn't let you walk away without meeting you." The rawness in his voice reached out to her, made her insides quiver. "Afterward, I decided to use whatever means necessary to hold onto you."

"Even if it meant lying?"

"Yes."

"That doesn't make you a very trustworthy person."

"I'm telling you the truth now."

Shawna looked away from the intensity of his gaze. Playing with the napkin on the tabletop, she berated herself for the bit of joy that filled her with his words. *I couldn't let you walk away.* Yet he had.

Head held high, she'd walked away with as much dignity as she could. Once out of view, she'd taken off running down the sidewalk, uncaring of the stares of strangers and the tears streaming down her cheeks. She'd only known she had to get back to the hotel and the privacy of her room so she could manage the unbearable pain of seeing him with another woman and the realization that what they'd shared had been a lie. She'd never felt pain like that before or since.

"You hurt me."

"I know."

"Were you ever going to tell me? Or was what we did some dirty little secret?"

"It wasn't dirty," he said forcefully. "I swear to you, I planned to tell you. When I saw you on Sunday, outside my brother's apartment, I intended to tell you then, but I didn't get the chance."

"How do I know you're telling me the truth now?"

"You don't. But it is the truth. I'll tell you the truth about anything. Just ask me. I know you have questions and I want to earn your trust. Ask me anything and I'll answer truthfully."

"Are you sure you want to do this?"

"Yes."

Shawna's fingers stilled on the napkin. "Did you love her?"

"The way I felt about her paled in comparison to the way I felt about you."

"Answer the question. Were you in love with her when you slept with me?"

"It's a terrible thing to say, but no, I didn't love her. I'd had my doubts before, but being with you made me realize that I didn't love her. I'd gone to Chicago to make a decision about my life and my relationship with Holly, and you helped me make it." He took a deep breath, as if bracing himself. "What else?"

"You said you broke up, but . . . did you ever sleep with her again?"

"Shawna . . ."

"You said I could ask you anything."

"Anything but that."

"Your response is my answer, but I want to hear you say it."

His eyes looked steadily into hers. "Yes."

She'd goaded him, yet now that he'd told her, the words tore at her insides. "Of course you did. You have quite the libido."

"It's not what you think. It only happened after I thought I'd never see you again, and I—"

"Thank goodness you didn't get our names mixed up."

"Shawna, listen to me."

"After I saw you with her, I kept telling myself it was a nightmare." She started to shake, could feel her control slipping away.

"Shawna."

"I didn't want to believe it had happened."

"I was young and stupid. I didn't know what to do. I didn't know how to handle the situation with both of you there."

"You never even called."

"I should have, right away, but I didn't know what to say, and I thought you hated me. I didn't think you'd accept a call from me."

"*I waited.*" The pain-filled words fell between them like a bomb, shutting down the back and forth. Her eyes dodged his. She hadn't meant to admit that. It came out and she wished she could take it back.

He reached across the table, but she pulled back before he could touch her, placing both hands in her lap. She couldn't stand it if he touched her. His touch wouldn't offer comfort— it would simply cause more pain in her emotional state.

His fingers curled into a fist on the tabletop. "I went to the hotel as soon as I could, but you had already left."

She looked across the table at him. "I never received a single message or a text from you."

He shook his head. "I gave up too easily." He leaned forward. "I'm sorry. I left The Haven Hotel and I wandered for a while. I couldn't face Holly or my brother. I didn't know what to do with myself. I'd screwed up everything. I never touched her in Chicago because that was *our* place. You and me. Holly and I argued, and I—"

"I'd rather not know the details, thank you." She still couldn't look at him. She had no right to feel envious. *She* had been the other woman, but for two nights he'd been hers, and the fact that he'd wound up back in Holly's arms opened a fresh wound.

"You should have never approached me that day on the street and make—" She'd almost admitted it. She'd almost said aloud what she'd hardly been able to say even to herself: *make me fall for you, make me need you.*

"I know I shouldn't have approached you, but to be honest, I didn't expect things to move so fast. Once we had dinner, I couldn't stop. I couldn't *not* spend time with you. Can you understand that at all? Can you comprehend a little bit of what I felt?"

She could. She understood it well because she'd been driven by the same desire to be with him. She didn't want to feel that way again because she didn't know herself when she was with him. It scared her.

Time to go. She started putting on her sweater.

"What are you doing?" Ryan asked in an alarmed voice.

"I'm leaving. I did what you asked. I had dinner with you."

"We haven't finished talking."

"There's nothing else to say."

"We have a lot of catching up to do. I have questions."

"I won't be answering them."

"What about you? Don't you have any more questions?"

She set her purse on her lap. "You answered the only one that I cared about."

"Shawna, I never touched her until we were back in Oklahoma—until I tried and couldn't reach you."

"I don't care. What's done is done and we can't go back. Okay? Let it go."

He shook his head, his jaw hardening with resolve. "I can't do that. I'm a different man than I was back then. You're right, I should have never approached you. I should have never lied when you asked me if I had a girlfriend. I was selfish. I was an ass. But everything I did was because I knew you were special and I felt that we could have something special. For a couple of days, I was the happiest I'd ever been in my life."

"I don't want to hear this."

"My life hasn't been the same since the day I met you."

Invisible fingers squeezed her heart tight. "*Don't.*"

"When I saw you tonight, I realized nothing had changed. Give me another shot, Shawna. I'm not the same man."

"I'm not the same foolish woman I was, either," Shawna said.

"We had a connection and you can't deny that."

"You're a liar, Ryan."

He swallowed. "Yes, but not about my feelings for you. Six years we've been apart. I can't let you walk out of my life again."

"Watch me."

"You have to forgive me. Please," he added with desperation, his eyes pleading.

Shawna rose from her chair, and the waitress picked that moment to come by the table. "Is everything all right over here?" she asked, looking from one to the other.

"We're fine," Ryan replied, keeping his gaze pinned on Shawna. He rose from his chair, too.

"My life is perfect, okay? No drama, no problems. I like my life the way it is."

"I'm not bringing any drama."

"Leave me alone, Ryan." At the hard note in her voice, the waitress eased away. "I never want to see you again. Stay away from me for good this time. Do you understand?"

She turned around and started walking away.

"Shawna, wait!"

She didn't slow down. She didn't turn. She kept on moving until she was safely out the door.

Chapter Twelve

Shawna pushed the key into her car's ignition and turned it. Nothing happened.

"Oh, no," she groaned. She tried repeatedly and then hit the steering wheel in frustration. Piece of junk car. It had been dependable when she bought it, but it was old now. She'd put off buying a new one, but she really needed a more dependable vehicle. If she didn't hate car shopping so much, she would've done it already.

She popped the hood and went around to the front. She examined the interior of the car, not even knowing what to look for. Of all the rotten times for the car to break down on her, it had to happen now, while she was frustrated and upset after running into the one man who made her feel like an incoherent preteen.

She cursed loudly.

"Need some help?" a voice asked.

Her heart jumped violently. Leaning to the

right so she could see around the hood, she saw the last person she wanted to see.

Ryan stood with his hip resting against the driver's door, his face partially hidden by a shadow cast by the parking lot light.

"Not from you," she replied.

That didn't stop him, of course. "I can't leave you out here to fend for yourself." He walked to her and rested his hands on the car, leaning in to take a look at the insides.

Shawna stepped away from him. "I'm a big girl. I'll be fine."

"Have you figured out what the problem is?"

"No, I'm not a mechanic."

"So what are you doing under here?"

"I thought I'd—look, I don't need your help, okay? I can call Triple A."

"What's it doing?"

Annoyed, Shawna quickly explained.

"It could be your battery," Ryan said.

Shawna frowned. "I bought a new battery less than a month ago."

"You could have gotten a bad one, or maybe it's your alternator. That drains the battery."

"Great."

"Why don't you call a tow truck to come get the car, and I'll give you a ride home?"

Her head snapped up. "I don't think so. I can easily call a taxi."

"Or I could give you a ride."

"I don't want a ride from you." Her voice grew firmer, making it clear she didn't want *anything* from him and preferred that he walk away.

She couldn't get rid of him that easily. "I won't make a move on you if that's what you're worried about. You've made it more than clear you don't want to have anything to do with me."

She eyed him suspiciously. "You're suddenly going to accept it?"

"Not accept it, but respect it. Let me help you."

"Don't do this, Ryan."

"Do what?"

"Be nice to me."

"Why?" His eyes mirrored the question. "I don't know any other way to be with you, Shawna."

His words tore a thin strip from her defenses. Staring off across the parking lot, she wrapped her arms around herself, pulling her sweater closer around her body.

"We can wait inside the restaurant or out here for the tow truck," Ryan said. "It'll probably be at least an hour. Once he gets here, you can decide if you want a lift home or not."

She didn't respond, her mind racing.

"I can't do anything you don't let me do," he said into the silence.

Her stomach trembled. Therein lay the problem. Seeing Ryan had awakened a storm of emotion, and she was more afraid of herself than him. She gnawed the inside of her cheek while he patiently waited.

"Fine," she said, heaving a sigh. "I'll call a tow truck, and then . . . then we'll see."

No emotion displayed on his face. He simply nodded, and she retrieved her purse from the car to make the call.

They stood in silence in the parking lot as they waited, both of them leaning their backs against her car.

Finally Ryan spoke. "I didn't mean to hurt you, but I didn't want to hurt Holly either," he said. "I couldn't just spring it on her. She and I had history."

"Is that the real reason, or were you worried about yourself?"

"A little bit of both." He looked over at her, but Shawna continued to stare across the parking lot. It gradually emptied as diners left for the night. "I broke things off with her. She didn't understand, and our families still wanted us together, which made it hard. She kept asking me questions, wanting to know if she'd done something wrong. One day, I admitted everything. And she forgave me." His laugh was hollow again, like in the restaurant. "Forgave me," he said quietly in disbelief. "That's when we slept together again. Because she forgave me and I needed to get you out of my mind. But it wasn't enough. When I finally ended it for good, she badmouthed me to all of our friends and family. She told everyone what I'd done, but I didn't care as much as I thought I would. I still felt terrible, but nothing mattered because I'd lost you." He sighed. "I swear, I never touched her again because she didn't deserve to be treated like a substitute for you, to help me forget you. I know you don't understand, but that's what happened."

"I do understand," Shawna said quietly. She'd done something similar when she moved to Atlanta. She'd met someone and used him to try to forget Ryan. It didn't work, and so she'd thrown herself into building her business. At least that had turned out to be successful.

She watched a couple exit the restaurant arm in arm and walk to a car before driving off.

"You still play pool?" Ryan asked in an effort to make conversation.

"On occasion, although I suck at it."

"Yeah, you do," he agreed, his voice sounding amused.

She swung her gaze around to him. "You're not supposed to agree with me."

He chuckled, the sound of his laughter way too attractive. "Why not? It's the truth, and we both know it."

Shawna straightened to her full height. "I did all right when we played those guys at the bar," she pointed out. "We beat them and won some money."

"Poor guys never stood a chance," Ryan murmured. "You distracted them in that dress."

That Saturday she'd purposely worn her white sundress dotted with images of red and green foliage on it. She liked the way the dress looked on her. It clipped around her neck, and the neckline dipped low on her breasts, showing off their fullness. The lightweight fabric skimmed her curves, and Ryan had spent the entire day with his hands lingering on some part of her body— her back, her shoulders, her bare arms. The halter top dress had been a distraction to him all day. He couldn't keep his hands off her, and she had basked in the heat of his constant attention.

That night, they'd gone to play pool and the

entire time they were in the pool room, he'd stood guard beside her like a sentry and stared down any man who dared look at her as she bent over the table to take her shots. At the end of the game, they collected their money and his fingers had curled around her wrist. Instead of walking out the front, he led her out a side door into an alley.

With a level of impatience she'd never seen any man exhibit before, he'd held her against the wall and growled in her ear that she'd been making him hard all day. They started slow and graduated to a passionate make-out session. His hands had roughly caressed her body, her fingers had tunneled into his hair, and their mouths had devoured each other with panting, hungry kisses. Soon, he'd been wedged between her thighs and had filled her, right there in the alley, with her knee hoisted above his waist.

The possibility of getting caught only heightened the level of eroticism. Even now, thinking back, she couldn't believe she'd done such a thing. She'd been into it—with him all the way, partially worried that someone would see them, but knowing they wouldn't stop even if they were caught.

No one had ever accused her of being spontaneous. She'd never uttered the words *go with the flow*. Yet with Ryan, none of it had mattered. She had been spontaneous. She had been uninhibited.

He, too, had seemed to learn something new about himself, because when they were done, he'd had a bewildered look on his face.

"Is something wrong?" she'd teased.

But he hadn't been amused. He'd simply stared at her for a while. So long, in fact, that she began to fidget. "No," he'd said. "Every-thing is finally right."

The words had warmed her. An unfortunately short-lived sensation.

"I had so much fun that weekend," Ryan said. "Felt like I didn't have a care in the world."

Shawna inhaled sharply and closed her eyes. Her heart started beating faster as she recalled the touch of his fingers, his breath on her neck.

Luckily, the flashing lights of the tow truck infiltrated her closed lids and the moment was lost. Beside her, Ryan shifted, and minutes later she gave the driver the address to her mechanic's shop.

Ryan asked her what she wanted to do, and for the second time that night she hovered in indecision. She could accept the lift from Ryan, but at what cost?

Finally, she decided she could handle him. The ride to her house wouldn't take long and then she could send him on his way and be done for the night.

"All I need is a lift, Ryan."

"That's all I'm offering."

Taking a much needed breath, Shawna followed Ryan across the parking lot to his blue pickup truck.

"Ready?" he asked after they put on their seat belts.

She pulled the bottom of her dress down to cover her legs as much as she could. No need to give him any ideas. Being inside the truck filled her with nervous energy. This heightened awareness of him signaled danger. She stayed close to the door so she couldn't smell him or be tempted to touch.

"Yes," she replied.

Chapter Thirteen

Neither of them said much as Ryan drove the truck toward Shawna's home in Buckhead.

She sat with her arms crossed, staring out the side window, when the vehicle began to slow down. To her surprise, Ryan pulled into the parking lot of a Krispy Kreme doughnut shop.

"What are you doing?"

"I'm getting doughnuts." He got in line behind two other vehicles.

"Is this really necessary?" she asked.

He looked calmly at her. "It won't take long. This is something I do sometimes after I leave work late. Thanks to you, I'm helplessly drawn to the 'Hot Now' sign." He looked anything but helpless.

The flashing red sign alerted passersby that the glazed doughnuts—the signature item—were hot and freshly made. Shawna stared at it since it was significantly less dangerous than looking at him.

Her stomach tightened as she remembered stopping at the store near Michigan Avenue and insisting he try one. They'd shamelessly gone through the box in the hotel room. When the last doughnut remained, they'd playfully fought over it. He'd been stronger and pinned her to the bed, but he offered to let her have it in exchange for a kiss. They'd then spent the next hour making love, the pastry completely forgotten.

Once Ryan placed the order and paid, he pulled out of the parking lot. Holding out the green and white box, he said, "You're welcome to have one."

Shawna could almost taste the sweet confection melting on her tongue. "No, thanks."

"Come on. You know you want one. You have just as bad of a sweet tooth as I do."

As if his cajoling tone wasn't enough, he waved the box under her nose. She smiled despite herself.

"Fine. But only one," she insisted, taking the box from him and opening it. Six freshly glazed doughnuts nestled against each other in the container.

Ryan chuckled. "Yeah, right." He took one and shoved most of it into his mouth.

"Slow down. You'll choke," she chastised him.

He shrugged. When he could speak, he said, "I've been hooked on them ever since that day we had them in Chicago. I swear they lace these things with crack. That's how they get you."

Shawna giggled. "I wouldn't doubt it."

He reached for another one and they ate in comfortable silence for a few minutes while the truck rolled slowly along the long road. When she finished the first one, Shawna sheepishly pulled another from the box. "I don't want them to go to waste," she explained.

"You're a martyr," Ryan said with amusement.

They smiled at each other and Shawna felt warmth in her chest. She didn't want that feeling. It meant she was getting comfortable with him. It meant she was enjoying spending time with him.

The white glaze covered the tips of her thumb and finger. The doughnuts were good but messy. She placed her thumb in her mouth, absentmindedly sucking off the icing.

"Now why'd you go and do that?" Ryan asked softly.

She turned to him. "Do what?"

"That," he replied, inclining his head toward her hand. "Now you have me wishing I was that finger."

An unbearable sensation crawled across her skin and awareness crackled between them.

Shawna cleared her throat. "I'll use a napkin," she muttered. "Please keep your eyes on the road." On edge, she continued talking to keep her mind off of being in such close quarters with him. "How's your mother?" Six years ago, his mother had been recovering from breast cancer.

"I told you about her?" he asked.

She nodded. "One time you mentioned her fight with cancer. You said you didn't know what your father would do if anything happened to her."

Ryan remained quiet for a moment before he answered. "She had a relapse a couple of years ago but beat it again. My dad fell apart, and the medical bills piling up made things worse."

"Did your brother have to step in to help again?"

"We both did this time. It surprised my father that I could actually contribute. He finally admitted that my decision to leave college wasn't a completely crazy idea."

"You can't live your life for other people. You made the right decision for you."

He looked over at her, a grateful smile on his face. "Thanks."

They said very few words the rest of the way to her house. Aside from her giving him the occasional instruction on where to turn to get there, the only sound in the truck was the soothing soft rock music coming through the speakers. She handed him her keycard so he could swipe it and let them into the small community—ten buildings with two townhouses in each. When they pulled up in front of her home, she hopped out of the vehicle.

Ryan turned off the engine. "I'll walk you to the door."

"That's not necessary."

"I don't mind."

Acutely aware of his soft footfalls behind her on the walkway, Shawna couldn't shake a feeling of déjà vu. At the front door, she rummaged in her purse for the keys. The sound of her searching fingers magnified in the quiet neighborhood. The darkness of the porch enveloped them. She would have to put replacing the burned out light bulb on her list of things to do because she kept forgetting. She finally pulled the key ring from her purse.

Shawna hesitated before placing the key in the door. She didn't want to appear ungrateful. She looked up at Ryan, feeling jittery and uneasy. He seemed bigger in the dark, with the moon and the night sky as a backdrop. "Thank you for bringing me home."

He leaned in close and she stopped breathing. His voice was soft, caressingly low when he spoke. "I'd do anything for you."

Ryan felt his body harden. The intimacy of the porch wreaked havoc on his senses, and so did knowing he stood outside her home. He'd told himself to back off, but he was right at it again.

She didn't respond, choosing to insert the key into the lock. The light from a pole in the parking lot cast a faint glow across her neck, and he wished he could press his lips against her tender flesh and listen to her soft little moans as she became aroused. He was so engrossed in his thoughts that a few seconds passed before he registered her struggle with the dead bolt.

"Is it stuck?" he asked.

"Yes. Sometimes it gets like that." She pushed and turned the key at the same time.

"You should get that fixed. Let me try."

Instead of allowing her to move aside so he could work on the door, he reached around her, enclosing her in his arms. Any excuse to be close to her. He heard her soft intake of breath. He stood as close to her as he possibly could without pressing his entire body into hers and letting her feel how much he wanted her. She stiffened as he placed his hand over the batch of keys, twisted, and pushed. The door gave.

"There," he said.

Neither of them moved and the temptation to press his face against the inviting crook of her neck and immerse himself in her smell overtook him.

Shawna felt his breath on her ear. Did he want to touch her as much as she wanted to be touched by him? Because right now she wanted to be made love to, the same way he'd made love to her before. The trembling fingers of one hand reached out to grasp the doorframe.

"Good night, Ryan."

She felt compelled to say that because she worried that if she didn't, she would invite him in. Part of her wanted him to come inside and remind her of what it was like to be blindingly out of control. Thoughts of him had lessened over the years, but she'd never truly forgotten him and what they'd shared.

His knuckles brushed the base of her spine and her skin prickled under his touch.

"I'm not leaving, Shawna," he said.

"What are you going to do? Stand out here?"

"No." His hand covered hers and stilled the trembling of her fingers.

"I'm not letting you in. You have to leave." A last-ditch effort to save face, but spending the night together had been inevitable from the minute she'd climbed into the truck with him.

"You don't want me to, and I don't want to." He rested his head against hers and whispered the next words. "I'm coming in."

Chapter Fourteen

They barely made it inside before Ryan was on her, the hard steel of his arousal straining against her backside in a restless grind. He was surprised it didn't tear through his suddenly too-snug jeans.

Grasping her from behind in the dark, he removed the sweater she had wrapped around her and tugged the ponytail holder from her hair to bury his fingers in the silky layers.

"I've been wanting to do that all night," he said in hoarse tones.

Shawna tilted back her head and his mouth landed on her luscious lips. Succulent. Tasty.

When she moaned, her sweet breath vibrated in his mouth. He gathered the hem of her dress in one fist, dragging it up past her thighs and causing her to shiver when his other hand glided in a firm caress over her hips to her stomach.

He loved her body—soft to the touch, womanly, and made for sex. He couldn't wait to get her naked so he would no longer have to suffer from a painful erection so swollen he didn't think he'd last long once he entered inside of her.

She turned in his arms, hot and desperate. Mouths still fused together, they stumbled into the wall. His tongue forged farther into her mouth and her fingertips drifted through his dark hair. Their tongues circled each other—stroking, teasing, and fanning the flames of desire.

Nibbling his lips, Shawna kissed him without restraint, blindly, eagerly. Sucking on his lower lip, licking his teeth, she relished the taste of him.

His hands kept busy. They were everywhere, like an octopus. A sexy, blue-eyed octopus who had her up against the wall and whose kisses created a painful ache deep in her abdomen. Ryan lowered his mouth to the skin of her neck, tormenting the arch of her throat down to the frantic pulse in the middle of her collarbone. He moved with a type of desperation, as if unable to resist kissing everywhere he saw exposed skin.

She tugged his shirt from the waistband of his jeans to touch him. The muscles of his back and chest jerked under her palms.

His hard thigh nudged her legs open. Shaking, she spread them wider so he could palm the damp silk of her panties. She made a sound of womanly approval as desire flooded between her thighs. Already spinning out of control, she burned up with a fever-like need.

A shaky gasp broke from her throat when one of his fingers penetrated the slick opening of her sex. Then another.

Ryan whispered in her ear, but she gasped and pumped so feverishly into his hand she didn't hear what he said. Arms wrapped around his neck, her breasts flattened against his chest, Shawna whispered his name over and over as her need raged on.

"Ryan . . . Ryan . . ."

As his fingers pumped inside of her, his thumb found the distended nub and massaged it. She came suddenly, violently, her feminine walls clutching at his fingers. An indecent amount of moisture flooded between her legs, and a thin trail of it slid along the inside of her thigh. It was that easy to get her off, as if her libido had simply been lying in wait for him to bring it back to full life.

He swore softly and she shut her eyes, tremors racing through her as her knees became as wobbly as gelatin, and she had to cling to him or collapse at his feet. Spearing his fingers into her loose hair, he held her against him. The tips of her breasts, enlarged and aching, tightened painfully in the close embrace.

"You only think about this every now and again?" he asked, reminding her of the answer she'd given when he asked if she ever thought about their time together. "How?"

This was the proof that she'd lied. The way she'd fallen into his arms, as if time and space hadn't separated them.

He dragged her into the living room toward the sofa, but they missed it and tumbled onto the floor. He took the brunt of the fall and she landed on top of him.

"You're so damn beautiful," he whispered, rolling her onto her back.

He found her mouth again and kissed her hungrily, then her cheeks, showering her with affection—alternating between soft and sweet, and hard and demanding. His mouth moved lower to her neck where he lingered for a moment, trailing hot kisses and nipping her skin just shy of too hard.

Quickly, he undid the buttons of her dress and popped the clasp at the front of her bra. Her freed breasts stood at attention, swollen and waiting for his next move. Caressing his neck, she guided him lower, aching for the heat of his breath, the flat of his tongue on her nipples. Finally, he kissed them, torturing the tips with the edge of his teeth.

"Yes, yes." She whispered encouragement as he moved from one to the other.

The sound of him unsnapping his pants sharpened the ache in her loins. She couldn't resist helping him push his boxers past his hips. And she couldn't resist touching him.

He sucked in a sharp breath when she reached for his heavy hardness, shaping the length and girth, recalling what it was like to have him inside of her. How he would make her senses reel and her breath catch with the strength of his thrusts. She stroked the veined exterior until he let loose a groan through clenched teeth.

"You have to stop, love . . . I can't . . ." He made a sound at the back of his throat and pushed away her hand. Within seconds, he sheathed his erection in a condom.

His hands went under her dress again, dragging aside the silky material of her panties. He trailed his fingers over the thatch of dark hair between her thighs, the feathered touch on the plump, wet folds almost making her come again.

He moved between her legs and his body claimed hers—the only appropriate word to describe the act. *Claim.* Like the planting of a flag on unchartered territory. That's how she felt with him. Like untouched, virgin land.

Her inner muscles adjusted to accommodate him, conforming to fit around his wide shaft. The pleasure of it was incomparable.

Ryan stretched her arms above her head, intertwining their fingers together. As he lowered his head to her chest, she arched off the floor, letting loose a gasping cry when his mouth fastened around a nipple. He sucked the dark bud, so sensitized now after becoming reacquainted with his mouth, sending a flash of need straight to her center. Every time he sucked, a throb echoed in her core, creating a rush of wetness between her thighs.

He showed no signs of easing up even as she trembled beneath him. Each thrust of his hips filled her, and she lifted upward in time to his movements, pulling him deeper into the silken heat of her sex. But she could sense him holding back, leashing the need to plunder her body with the passion she craved.

Ryan lifted his head, the set of his jaw hard as he suffered behind a wall of restraint. "You're so wet for me," he said. "I want to go slow, but . . ."

Shawna shook her head wildly. That's not

what she wanted right now. Not when she felt so frantic, could feel the pulse of his hard flesh deep inside of her. "Don't go slow. Go fast. Go hard. Go . . . just . . . *go* . . ."

He needed to hear that. He let loose a series of thrusts that pushed her along the floor. Wherever bare skin met the carpet, it burned, bruising her flesh. But she didn't want him to stop because it was unbearably good. Her body reawakened and accepted the fiery sensations—the type of sensations that blurred the lines between pain and pleasure.

He'd ruined her for any other man. She'd hoped that her mind had created a false memory of how amazing it had been between them, but tonight's reality surpassed the recollection.

Legs spread wide, she was pinned beneath him and filled to capacity. Unable to move, unable to escape as he drilled into her. He controlled her with each thrust, damn near stamping his name on her privates—in all caps, bolded, so she'd never forget who it belonged to. Sex had never been this good, this untamed with anyone else. She screamed from the intensity of it, begging him to stop *and* not stop, all in the same breath.

Lying there, panting and groaning, they were the perfect example of lusty impatience. Both still wearing all their clothes, right down to their underwear—rutting around on the carpet in heat.

The need for him filled her with pain and Shawna longed for relief. Gripping his hips between her thighs, her body rocked back and forth in search of it. Desire twisted inside of her and her toes curled at the base of his spine. A sound of pure bliss surfaced in her throat and emerged as a wild moan.

The room spun when a series of earth-shattering orgasms rattled through her. The whole house seemed to rock with the impact of the tremors.

Mere moments later, Ryan surged within her. He began thrusting harder, his path eased by the wetness only he could inspire—once, twice—and then he uttered a deep groan, bowing his head to her shoulder as the same seismic vibrations overtook him.

When it was over, their heavy, breathless panting could be heard in the dark room. Ryan continued to hold onto her hands, still stretched above her head.

The short session had only whetted Shawna's appetite. She looked at him with renewed desire.

"I never forgot you," she whispered.

Their gazes locked. "I never forgot you, either, love. You're my everything. *Every*thing."

With their faces so close together, she could clearly see his expression. Fierce hunger darkened his eyes.

"Take me upstairs," she said.

He pulled up his pants and lifted her from the floor. They spent the rest of the night getting reacquainted.

Chapter Fifteen

Ryan awoke with a start and sat up, his subconscious alerting him that he wasn't in his own bed. He looked around the small space and gradually his memory came back.

Shawna's bedroom.

He rubbed the sleep from his eyes and swung his legs off the bed, squinting at the sun coming in through the window. She must be downstairs already because he didn't hear her in the adjoining bathroom.

Smiling to himself, he stood up, thinking about the night before.

Shawna.

He was behaving like a man experiencing his first love, but it might be an accurate description. He'd never felt this way about anyone.

The experience with Shawna in Chicago had become the benchmark by which he measured every other woman. It didn't make sense when he considered they'd only had those two days, but no other woman had ever made him feel such an intense attraction. Not a single one, and it wasn't for lack of trying to recapture the feeling.

One by one, he lifted his clothes from the floor and put them on. He went downstairs and found her in the kitchen wearing a white silk robe, looking out the window over the sink. He walked toward her.

"Good morning," he said.

"Morning," she greeted over her shoulder. He knew what she was doing. Overthinking, overanalyzing.

Shawna sipped her coffee, reliving what had happened and hiding from her feelings and what she'd done. She'd been so caught up, not bothering to think about what it all meant. This morning she'd woken up and tried to figure out if this meant they were a couple, or was this one of those odd reconnects with no real definition. And if so, could she handle it?

She considered her life as near to perfect as it could be. She owned her own place in an exclusive part of town, she had a successful business and a clique of close girlfriends she could call on any time she needed companionship. But Ryan added a dimension she hadn't anticipated, and it threatened to disrupt her peaceful life.

She wanted to do the modern thing and act as if sleeping with him had been no big deal, but it *was* a big deal to her.

"Coffee?" she asked.

"No." She heard him come closer. "Can I tell you what I really want this morning?"

"Sure. Would you prefer tea or juice?"

"Neither," he said quietly. "I'd rather have you."

Shawna closed her eyes and tightened her fingers around the mug before carefully setting it on top of the counter. "You had me last night," she said in an effort to resist the inevitable outcome.

"I want you this morning, too." He grasped the back of her neck, and she shivered at his touch. His rough thumb moved back and forth over her skin. He pressed against her, his erection hard and long against her backside. "You feel that?" he said, his voice a husky whisper. "This is me all the time, every time I'm near you. I can't keep my hands off of you."

They had a similar problem. She'd been aroused long before he even touched her. She remained in a constant state of arousal around him. Closing her eyes, Shawna fought back the moan building up in her chest.

Her head fell back and he kissed the underside of her jaw.

She touched his rough cheek with the backs of her fingers, turning her head so he could kiss the corner of her mouth. The silk of her robe brushed along her inner thigh, feeling way too sensual in a way it never had before.

Was there no end to the ways in which he affected her?

Turning around, her eyes sought his, seeking some kind of answer, but finding only the lazy smile that seemed to hover perpetually around his mouth.

He unfastened the belt and slid the robe from her shoulders, letting his hand glide along her arms on its way down. A heavy heat settled between her thighs as she watched his appreciative gaze scan her naked form, his eyes darkening to cobalt blue as he pulled her closer.

She slid a hand around his neck and dragged his head down to hers. Their kiss deepened, and she lost the ability to think. But thinking could come later.

Right now, she only wanted to *feel*.

****

Shawna awoke slowly. The curtains were closed so no light came in. She'd fallen asleep after she and Ryan made love again.

She looked around the room in search of him, and her gaze landed on a note propped against the lamp beside the bed. He'd torn a page from her small pad on the desk in the corner.

Had to go into the shop. I'll call you later.

She lifted the piece of paper and ran her finger over it. She'd never seen his handwriting before. He wrote with a bold and heavy script. Masculine, like him.

The house phone beside the bed rang and she answered after checking the caller I.D.

"Why haven't you called to tell me what happened last night? Am I going to have to beat it out of you?" Yvonne asked. She could tell her sister was in the car and heard her niece and nephew talking in the back seat.

"Whatever happened to hello?" Shawna asked, stretching and stifling a yawn. She placed the note back on the bedside table and sat up against the pile of pillows. She really needed to get her butt out of bed but felt extra lazy this Saturday morning. Good sex and plenty of orgasms could do that to a person. The boutique was in good hands with her employees, but she'd check on them after she ended the call.

"Since we're sisters, we're not limited to such formalities," Yvonne said. "Now spill it."

"We had a nice time," Shawna said cautiously, wondering how much she should divulge.

"Hmm. That's vague." Yvonne paused. "William thinks he's a great guy and when I met him, I thought so, too. But how do you feel about him?"

"He's fine."

"Did you have a serious relationship in Chicago? You never told me about him."

"That's because it wasn't serious." Shawna dreaded the fallout from her next words. "We met right before I left Chicago, and um . . . he had a girlfriend he didn't tell me about."

"What! I remember you didn't seem like yourself when you came home. Why didn't you tell me? I'm so sorry. If I'd known I wouldn't have set you up on a date with him."

"Don't worry about it."

"Are you sure?"

"Yes."

"How did you feel when you saw him again?"

Shawna shrugged though her sister couldn't see her. "Angry at first, but then . . ." *Shaky, desperate, achy.*

"But then . . . ?"

She might as well confess everything. "We had

sex." She heard a series of car horn honks and sat up in alarm. "Yvonne, are you there? Is everything okay?"

"I have my babies in the car. You can't spring stuff like that on me while I'm driving. Plus, I'm pregnant." Yvonne had a habit of using her pregnancy as an excuse for every mishap, miscommunication, or mishandling of any situation. "Are you guys okay back there?"

"Yes, Mommy!"

"What does being pregnant have to do with anything?"

"You've never been pregnant, so you wouldn't understand. I take it you're going to continue seeing him?"

"Yes, but I want to take things slow." She rushed on to thwart the snappy comment she knew her sister would make. "I can still take it slow even though we've already slept together. Who knows, maybe we can keep it physical and enjoy each other for now."

"You're not the kind to have S-E-X and remain detached, so don't pretend that you are." Yvonne had lowered her voice so the kids couldn't hear her in the back.

Shawna flopped back against the pillows. "Can I please have my moment?"

"No, because you're being ridiculous. If you've already done you-know-what, it's obvious you have strong feelings for him. Why not go with it?"

"I'm not jumping into a serious relationship with the first man I've started seeing in months." She didn't even know if Ryan wanted a relationship. "There are plenty of other men out there I could date."

"Like who?"

"They're out there."

"First you complain there are no available men—wait a minute, he is available now, isn't he?"

"Yes." At least that's what he'd said. Surely he wouldn't lie to her about that twice.

"Now you have a man who's interested and you want to take it slow. But you've already had you-know-what with him. I think that ship has sailed, honey."

"I don't need your voice of reason right now."

"And what about Jerome?"

Shawna plucked at the sheet. "What about him? There's nothing going on between us. We're friends, that's all." She and Jerome had dated a few times, but it hadn't work out.

"He's your neighbor and he's going to see Ryan coming and going."

"*And . . . ?* I've dated other men since Jerome and I broke up. Besides, we're friends."

"He's always so helpful, lurking around—"

"Lurking?"

"—acting like his only concern is being a good neighbor. I don't trust him. No man hangs around like that without an ulterior motive. At least that's what William said, and he's a man so he should know."

"We talked after we stopped dating, and we both agreed we were better off as friends. Sometimes he can be a little pushy, but it's hard to cut him off when he's been so nice to me. I wouldn't want to hurt his feelings."

"You know what your problem is?"

"I'm sure you'll tell me."

"You're too nice."

"There's no such thing."

"Yes, there is. You're a perfect example of it."

"Are you done?"

"For now." Shawna heard the worry in her sister's voice when she spoke next. "One last thing. I know I joke a lot, but be careful with Ryan. I don't want to see you get hurt, and I'll feel terrible if I had any part in it because I got you two back together. You say you want to take things slow, but it doesn't seem like you have. You seem to be all in with this guy already. I hope you know what you're doing."

Shawna had the same concerns as Yvonne—that she was in over her head, and they both knew she wasn't much of a risk-taker.

"I hope I know what I'm doing, too," she admitted.

Chapter Sixteen

"Take it easy, guys," Ryan said.

He stood back and watched the commercial movers wrangle the large conference table into the trailer of the moving truck. Technically, his shop was closed on Saturdays, but he'd made an exception today. The law firm of Benson & Gates had requested the table for the conference room. He'd also designed and created a matching credenza, as well as office furniture for one of the partners. They wanted everything moved into their new building over the weekend so as not to disrupt the office.

As much as he wanted the movers to hurry so he could get back to Shawna, he didn't want them rushing and causing any damage to his product. He was proud of the pieces. He'd worked on them himself and they were some of his best work.

For the attorneys, money had been no object,

so he'd imported genuine mahogany wood from South America through an importer with a reputable supplier. He'd polished the reddish-brown surface of each piece to a high gleam and expected nothing except satisfaction—and hopefully referrals that would help grow his business.

Fifteen minutes later, Ryan leaned against his truck and dialed Shawna's number. He looked forward to hearing her voice and spending more time with her today. Except when he called, she didn't have the level of enthusiasm he expected when he suggested they meet up.

"I have a million things to do," she said. "I have to find a car. It turns out mine is kaput. My mechanic said he'd love to keep taking my money, but he doesn't advise putting any more into the car, so I've got to start car shopping today."

"I can help you with that. I can take you around."

"There's no need," she responded. "Months ago I created a spreadsheet with the different car options, and I pretty much know which one I need to get. I've avoided going, but I'll visit a few dealerships today to see what they have in stock and test drive the cars I'm interested in. It's nothing I can't do myself."

Her words disappointed him, but he tried not to let it bother him. He thought about how he'd left her that morning, sound asleep after a bout of passionate lovemaking. "I could come by tonight and we could take up where we left off. I—"

"I'll probably be tired from car shopping, so tonight's not a good night."

He tried to come up with another reason to see her, but he suspected she'd have an excuse for why he couldn't. "What's going on, Shawna?"

The other end of the line remained silent. Finally, she let out a small breath. "Everything is moving so fast."

She was scared, which was understandable. Hell, the way he felt about her scared him, too. "What do you want to do?"

"Slow down."

His mind rejected that answer, and he swallowed the bitterness of it. "What does that mean?"

"I need a little bit of space. It's too much too soon."

Ryan stepped away from the truck and paced the gravel yard.

"Are you there?"

He stopped the restless movement. "Yeah, I'm here."

"You understand, don't you?"

Her voice sounded hesitant, and he could almost see the uncertainty in her eyes. "No, I don't, but I don't want to crowd you."

More silence, which he didn't know how to fill with any meaningful words to convince her to change her mind. Nothing would be gained by slowing down their relationship. Whatever she feared wouldn't disappear because they didn't see each other today or tomorrow.

They *were* moving fast, and he recognized the unnaturalness of it for her. She planned everything and felt most comfortable doing things by the book. Ever since high school when she'd fallen in love with fashion, she'd been determined to own a boutique and had taken the necessary steps to make sure that she not only achieved that goal, but that she succeeded at it.

He, on the other, lived life by the seat of his pants. He'd vacillated in college, changing his major several times before settling on information systems, and then dropped out when he finally figured out where his passion lay. One minute he was in college, the next he was building furniture. One minute he lived in Oklahoma, the next he'd moved to Georgia to buy a business and start over.

"Thank you for understanding," Shawna said.

"I'm leaving town next Friday to go home to Oklahoma," he said. He wanted to invite her to come with him, but she'd probably freak. "My baby sister's coming home for spring break and since I haven't been home for a while, I thought this would be a good time to go."

"How long will you be gone?"

"A full week plus a couple of days."

"Okay."

She didn't have anything else to say? For him, a week without her sounded like a week in the desert without water. But for her, it was 'Okay.'"

"I want to see you before I leave," he said. "This space you need, I'll give it to you, but don't expect me to disappear." He'd let her go once and had never forgiven himself for it. She couldn't get rid of him that easily.

"Ryan—"

"I mean it."

Silence. "All right. Look, I better go. We can catch up later."

"I'll be in touch."

"Okay."

After they hung up, Ryan stared off into the distance, doing his best to not think about the disappointing conversation.

Okay.

He hated that word.

****

It took every bit of willpower Ryan had not to call Shawna on Sunday, but he'd promised to give her space and wanted to keep his promise. To do that, he went to his usual Sunday afternoon haunt, a local bar where he now sat with his friend, Tomas Molina.

Ryan nursed a mug of beer, watching Tomas flirt with the female bartender. He said something that made her blush and laugh. If dating were an Olympic sport, the Cuban immigrant would easily land the gold medal. A big, brawny guy with long brown hair, he went through women the way most men changed underwear and could often be heard doling out relationship advice to men and women in the bar. Why anyone would listen to the serial dater, Ryan couldn't understand.

"So what did William say when you told him you'd slept with his sister-in-law?" Tomas asked. He had a basket of wings in front of him and went through them as if they were his last meal.

"I didn't exactly tell him. I don't know how much information Shawna plans to share about Chicago or Friday night, and I don't want to make things awkward for her. He read between the lines and made it clear I'd have to answer to him if she got hurt."

Tomas nodded. "Understandable that he'd be protective."

"Yeah, but I wish he hadn't mentioned the part about being a doctor and knowing twenty different ways to slowly kill me with poison and not leave a trace."

Tomas choked on a piece of chicken and Ryan slapped his back. "He said that?" he asked once he'd caught his breath.

"Yes."

"You better be on your best behavior then, *amigo*."

Ryan frowned into his mug of ale. "I *am* on my best behavior, but I don't know if it'll do any good."

Tomas looked at him questioningly.

"She wants *space*," Ryan said.

"Space?" Tomas repeated the word like it was dirty. He wiped his hand on a napkin. "Let me tell you something about women," he said.

Ryan groaned. "No, please . . ."

"No really, listen to me."

"No, you listen. I screwed up once before, and this time I'm straight shooting with her. Whatever game you're going to suggest I play, I'm not interested. I don't want to play games."

"It's all games, but that's not what I'm about to tell you." Tomas's accent thickened at this point. There were only two times Ryan could think of when that happened: when he flirted with a woman and when he was serious. "Women always focus on the wrong things. For instance, no matter what you say, they're obsessed with their weight. They're either too skinny or too fat. Mostly they think they're too fat—even the skinny ones. What they should really be worried about is all the nagging and talking they do, especially when you're trying to get some rest or watch the game on TV. Or God forbid you're on a long distance call with your family and can't give them the attention they think they deserve." He muttered something in Spanish.

"Is this still about me?"

"Listen, women analyze every action, every comment. They drive us, and themselves, crazy trying to interpret our actions and words, instead of accepting them for what they are. The longer you're with them, the worse it gets. That's why I don't stick around long."

"You do realize you're messing it up for the next guy when you do that to these women?"

"His problem, not mine." Tomas took a large gulp of beer. "As I said, women focus on the wrong things, so you have to get Shawna refocused. You have to make her feel the same way she felt when she met you in Chicago. Take the focus off the negative part of your relationship—the bad ending—and remind her of the positive. While men get comfortable in a relationship, women are always trying to get back to that initial feeling—the excitement of when they first fell for you. That's why being with them is so much work." He muttered in Spanish again. "If you can get her back to that feeling, she'll be eating out of your hand."

Easier said than done, but it did make a little bit of sense. "You might be right." Ryan looked at his friend with new eyes. Maybe he really did know what he was talking about.

"Of course I'm right. Think back to what you did to make her fall for you."

Tomas had a point. Somehow he had to make Shawna feel comfortable with him again and set aside her reservations.

"Did you love her?" she'd asked, wanting to know if he'd been in love with Holly and still capable of making love to her.

"Excuse me," Tomas said to the bartender. "I'll take another beer, and I'd like to buy the lady at the end another glass of whatever she's having."

Ryan shook his head. Definitely a gold medalist.

He watched the television monitor above the bar. The combustible chemistry between him and Shawna made him feel he needed to wear heat resistant coveralls around her. He guessed that was part of the problem. He needed to prove to her more than just sex existed between them, even though it consisted of a mind-blowing variety he'd never experienced before her.

Although the speed at which their relationship had progressed suited him, if she felt they were moving too fast, he could slow down to match her pace. A little self-control could go a long way toward proving to her that they had something special, and she didn't have to worry about being hurt by him again.

The bartender placed Tomas's beer on the

counter and handed him a folded napkin. "She gave you her number."

Tomas frowned when he unfolded it. "There are two numbers on here."

"The second one is mine." She winked and walked away to tend to another patron.

Smiling, Tomas tucked the napkin into his shirt pocket and turned to Ryan. "I love this country."

Chapter Seventeen

Outside her boutique, La Petite Robe, Shawna checked the window displays on either side of the door and made a mental note to have Erin switch out a few items to showcase more of the seasonal picks.

She employed Erin, one of two full-time employees, and a part-timer. All her staff trained as personal shoppers, a key component to helping her build her business. She kept an extensive file on regular customers she referred to as clients. Staff noted their style, color preferences, and sizes, and each salesperson called the client assigned to them whenever items arrived in the store that might be of interest.

They'd been open a couple of hours and a few customers browsed inside the store. Shawna pointed out items on clearance before she continued to the back.

Erin looked up from dressing a mannequin.

"Good morning. How's the car?"

Shawna had purchased a Camry over the weekend. "I love it. I don't know why I took so long to get a new one, but I'm glad I finally did it. It's a relief not having to worry about whether or not my car will start when I turn the key."

"It's a major purchase. I understand why you took your time."

Her sister hadn't felt the same. Yvonne had given her a hard time, stating she couldn't comprehend why she hadn't bought a new car sooner when she'd probably spent the equivalent of a new car in clothes and shoes in the past year. Yvonne didn't "get" her obsession.

Erin looked past her toward the front of the store. "What's that?"

Shawna turned around to see a man striding down the middle aisle with a bouquet of red roses and a small box wrapped in white paper and gold ribbon.

"Shawna Ferguson?" he asked.

"Yes. I'm Shawna."

"These are for you."

Shawna signed for the items and read the card. Erin tried to peer over her shoulder, but Shawna moved so she couldn't see.

Remember the first night we went out? I want to create more memories like that. Ryan

"What's this all about?" Erin asked. "Have you been holding out on me?"

"Mind your business and get back to work."

"No, you have to—" Erin broke off when the store phone rang behind the counter.

"You better get that," Shawna said.

"We're not done!" Erin called as Shawna hurried away.

She entered the small office located at the back of the store. After she set the flowers on the edge of the desk, she tore off the gift wrap to find an MP3 player and earbuds nestled in cotton.

"What are you up to, Ryan?" she asked the empty room.

She put in the earbuds and turned on the device. As she listened, a slow smile spread across her face. A compilation of the eighties and nineties songs she and Ryan had danced to that Friday night in Chicago played in her ears.

She didn't know how long she sat there, listening to the music, bobbing her head and reminiscing about the party and his surprisingly good moves on the dance floor. She continued to listen as she answered e-mail and updated the store blog.

She only stopped to speak on the phone, place an order, and speak to a couple of clients. Around noon, her cell phone rang, and she fished it out of her bag. Ryan.

"Did you get my surprise?" he asked.

"Yes." She bit her lip.

"You're smiling."

"How do you know?"

"I can hear it in your voice."

With her elbow on the table, she rested her chin on her hand. "Yes, I'm smiling. But you know this was corny."

"Yeah, but you like it." Her smile broadened and she didn't deny it. "I wanted you to know I was thinking about you."

"Thank you."

"I meant what I said in the note, too. I want us to create more memories together." Without waiting for a response, he shifted gears. "Did you get a new car?" She answered in the affirmative and told him about it. "Now you don't have to worry about being stranded somewhere."

"True. I should've done it a long time ago."

"Well, I better get back to work." He sounded reluctant to hang up. "Keep a look-out. There are a few more things coming your way."

"You don't have to do that."

"I want to. I'll talk to you tomorrow."

Before hanging up, she wanted to let him know how much she appreciated the gifts. "Ryan, I love the flowers, and I really enjoyed the music. It brought back good memories."

"I'm glad to hear it."

Before the store closed, a second delivery arrived. Another bouquet of roses, this time accompanied by a box of Krispy Kreme doughnuts. She laughed when she saw them, wondering how in the world he'd arranged it. They weren't 'Hot Now,' but almost as good.

Shawna couldn't put off Erin after that. As they devoured the sugary treat, she gave her only a quick summary. Being a private person, she didn't want to divulge too much, and certainly not to an employee. She told her she'd reconnected with an old flame and left it at that.

****

The next day, Shawna sat in the back office placing orders before she ran to lunch. Most of the time she ordered a few sizes of the same outfit, but she liked one black and white dress so much, she ordered an extra one for herself.

It'll be sad if I go broke running this store, she thought.

"*Shawna.*" Erin sang her name from the open door, a sly look on her face. "You have another delivery. This time it's a *special* delivery."

Right behind her, Ryan appeared in the doorway. Her heart jumped at his unexpected visit. Erin slinked away, and Shawna stood up. "What are you doing here?"

He closed the door and sauntered over.

"It's been three days, and I stayed away as long as I could. I wanted to see you." His low, sexy voice caused her pulse to flutter. He took a few minutes to drink her in before pulling his arm from behind his back and revealing another bouquet. Tulips this time.

"More flowers?" Shawna said, smiling. One vase of roses sat on the far corner of her desk, and the other on a file cabinet against the wall. Their sweet aroma filled the small space. "How many are you going to buy?"

"As many as I need to." He walked around the desk and brought them to her.

"Thank you," she said, taking them.

He tilted his head. "Look at all this space between us. There's a good, what, two feet right now?"

Shawna laughed and shook her head. "And why did you mention that?"

He stopped smiling. "Well, you said you wanted space, but I really want to kiss you right now. I think I should get a little reward, don't you?"

"A little one," Shawna whispered.

Ryan stepped closer and lowered his head. They both moaned when their lips touched. His hand moved to the back of her head, and he slid his mouth over her mouth in the softest of kisses. His lips caressed the corner of hers, and she whimpered, slipping out the tip of her tongue to tease his lower lip.

He lifted his head and drew a shaky breath. She could clearly see the heat in his eyes and knew he saw the same in hers. "Stop trying to seduce me," he said softly.

"I am not."

"It sure felt that way," he said. "Behave yourself."

Shawna pushed him playfully and he laughed.

"Let's go out tomorrow," he said. "How about an action movie? I can come pick you up after I leave work."

"A movie? Tomorrow's the middle of the week."

"I have a secret to tell you," Ryan said, lowering his voice. She strained to hear him. "People go to the movies during the week, too."

She shook her head at him. "Why do I get the feeling you won't take no for an answer?"

"Because I won't take no for an answer."

"In that case, my answer is yes."

"Good. I'll see you tomorrow around eight."

"Thank you for the flowers," she said, as he walked to the door.

He paused and looked at her for a long moment. "Thank you for the kiss."

After he left, Shawna sniffed the tulips and

stared at them for a long time before she realized what she was doing—and that except for when they kissed, the smile hadn't left her face the entire time he'd been there.

Chapter Eighteen

Outside Shawna's townhouse, Ryan pulled his truck next to her numbered parking space and her shiny new Camry. It wasn't a racy red or a sleek black. She'd chosen beige—a non-assuming color that didn't draw attention to itself but fit her personality perfectly.

He exited his truck and walked toward her townhouse, casting his glance around to the buildings on either side. Someone in the building to the right quickly pulled the curtains back in place when he looked in that direction.

He liked the idea that Shawna had nosy neighbors. They always noticed unfamiliar faces and could be counted on to call the police. Although she lived in a nice community, one couldn't be too careful nowadays.

When Shawna opened the door, he took in the sight she made, taking a deep breath and drawing in the light scent of her perfume. She wore her hair in a ponytail, with the bangs dipping down to her eyebrows.

Even dressed simply, she impressed in a pair of jeans and a purple three-quarter-sleeved blouse that draped off her left shoulder. He'd be kissing that bare shoulder later tonight. Her jewelry included a large necklace and big round earrings.

"Right on time," she said.

He leaned in and drew her close because he couldn't help it. She didn't resist, so he kissed her lips and then kissed her exposed shoulder. Okay, so he couldn't wait until later.

"Are you ready to go?" she asked, touching his face.

He thought about saying no, that he'd rather stay in and undress her. From the longing in her eyes, she wouldn't have minded. But he'd promised to take her to a movie and that's what he intended to do, if for no other reason than to prove there was more than just sex between them.

"Sure," he said. She grabbed her purse, and as she shut the door, he asked, "Have you gotten that door fixed?"

"Not yet. I'll get someone to look at it soon."

"Here, let me look at it." Ryan pushed it back open and turned on the light in the foyer. He crouched down in front of the lock and examined the deadbolt, twisting it left and right. "Hmm . . ."

"What is it?" She stood over him.

"Looks like the latch is lining up fine with the plate, but it may need a little lubrication. I have some WD-40 in the truck. It'll only take a few minutes, and then we can leave."

He retrieved the can. When he came back, he swung the door inward and crouched down in front of it again, intending to spray into the holes.

"Hey there, neighbor."

Ryan looked up to see a black male coming up the steps. He had a low-cut Afro with flecks of gray at the temples and wore an expensive jogging suit with brand new tennis shoes.

"Hi, Jerome."

"You look lovely." His gaze traveled over Shawna in a more-than-neighborly fashion. The muscles in Ryan's shoulders tensed. "I see you finally hired some help," the man continued. "I guess you don't need me anymore."

"Ryan's not maintenance. He's . . . a friend."

Still in the crouched position, Ryan glanced at Shawna. Okay, fair enough, they hadn't defined their relationship yet, but they were more than friends. And what a facetious comment from this guy, because he had to know it was highly unlikely hired help would be working on Shawna's door this time of night.

"I've known Shawna for a while," Jerome said. "I've never seen you before."

Ryan rose from his position and stood to face the man, with Shawna on his right between them. "Well, you can expect to see me much more often."

Jerome raised his eyebrows. "I see. Well, if you're not a handyman, what is it that you do?" He looked him over with a certain insolence that suggested whatever Ryan did would never be up to par. It didn't faze Ryan. He'd had his share of people looking down their noses at him because he tended to wear jeans and had a nontraditional job. Men like Jerome annoyed more than upset him, but Jerome's relationship with Shawna disquieted him.

"I make custom furniture. And you?"

"I'm an attorney," Jerome said, a certain authoritative tone to his voice. He even seemed to stand up straighter. "It was nice to meet you, Ryan, and if you're a friend of Shawna's, you're a friend of mine."

"Actually, Shawna and I are a little more than friends." Ryan slipped his arm around her shoulders. She stiffened and looked up at him, but he watched Jerome's reaction and wasn't surprised when he saw jealousy surface in the other man's eyes as he honed in on Ryan's arm.

"I didn't mean to step on any toes," Jerome said smoothly. "Shawna and I have been friends about two years now, and we help each other out every now and again."

"Mostly you help me, and I appreciate everything you do," Shawna said.

"Help with what?" Ryan asked.

"Nothing much," Jerome replied. "I do little things for her, like help her move furniture or even something as simple as replacing the light bulb on her porch." He looked pointedly at Shawna.

She groaned. "I know, I need to go to the hardware store and pick up the light bulb."

"When you buy it, let me know, and I'll bring over my step ladder and install it for you like I did last time."

"No need," Ryan interjected. "I'll help her with that."

"Of course." Jerome's smiled tightly. "I'll leave you two alone. Have a good evening."

Ryan watched him walk down the steps and turn toward the building where he'd noticed someone peeking through the curtain. Shawna closed the door and locked up.

They were both silent as they descended the steps. The cool night air brushed over them on the way to Ryan's truck.

"Shawna, one more thing," Jerome called out. "We're still on a week from Saturday, right?"

"Uh, yes." She actually looked uncomfortable.

"Good. Our law firm is having a party," he explained to Ryan. "We recently bought a new building. Saturday night is the night we chose to do sort of a pre-open-house open house to show it off to friends and family." He refocused on Shawna. "We'll catch up about the details next week. Goodbye, Ryan."

Ryan and Shawna continued to his truck and remained silent until he'd pulled out of the parking lot.

"Did you have to make that comment back there about us being more than friends?" Shawna asked.

"We are."

"I don't need my business broadcast to everyone in my neighborhood."

"It was only Jerome."

"My private life is private and I didn't like it when you said that. I don't even know what that means—more than friends."

"It means I don't want you to go to a party with him on Saturday night. Does that clarify it for you?" Ryan gripped the steering wheel.

"It's not a date, Ryan, and we made those plans months ago." She sounded annoyed.

"If you dress up and go out with a man who's not related to you, it's a date. Were you even going to tell me?"

"Tell you what? That I'm going out with one of my friends? You won't even be in town that weekend."

He looked at her out of the corner of his eyes. Her arms were crossed. "Did you ever have more than a friendship with him?"

"Why do you ask?"

"Is that a yes or a no?"

"Yes, I did. We went out a few times."

"Did you have sex with him?"

She heaved a sigh of annoyance. "Where is this going? He's a friend."

"Yes or no, Shawna?"

"No! Do you want to know about all my past relationships now?"

The cabin remained quiet as the truck rolled through the next few traffic lights. Shawna stared out the side window and Ryan tried, but failed, not to let his jealousy spoil what should have been a nice night out.

"I don't want you to go out with him."

"I'm not going to cancel on him last-minute."

"It's not last-minute. He'll have over a week to find a new date."

"Are you seriously asking me to do this?" Her eyes widened with surprise.

"Yes, I am."

"That's kind of ridiculous, don't you think?"

Their gazes collided. "You're doing this to spite me, aren't you?"

"Yes, because when I made these plans months ago, I knew you'd surprise me and come back into my life."

Silence.

"You're not even interested in him."

"I never said I was, and if you know that, why are you making a big deal out of it?"

"Because of him. He's interested in you. I can tell."

"Even if he is, nothing's going to happen between us. He's a friend."

"He wants to be more," Ryan said, his voice hardening.

"I don't want to argue."

"This isn't an argument. We're having a conversation about why you shouldn't be going out with Jerome."

"You know what? I'm not going to let someone who recently came into my life tell me what to do and with whom to do it. Turn the truck around."

"What?"

"Turn it around! I don't want to go to the movies anymore. I want to go home."

"I'm not taking you home."

"You might as well take me home now, because if you don't, the minute we get to the theater I'm going to call a cab." Her eyes challenged his before he looked away.

"Fine." Ryan gritted his teeth and swung the truck in a U-turn in the middle of the street.

"Are you insane?" Shawna screamed at him.

"You said you want to go home, so I'm taking you home. There's no pleasing you, is there?"

Shawna fell silent and stared out of the window, fuming. That fast, the evening had deteriorated. When he parked his truck at her house, she immediately jumped out.

"Would you wait a damn minute?" Ryan said.

"I have nothing to say to you," Shawna hissed. "You don't own me, Ryan, and I'll do as I please."

"What do you think you're doing?" he asked.

"I could ask you the same question."

"I'm asking you to respect my request."

"And I'm asking you to back off. This is why I need space. Because you're too intense." She marched up the wooden stairs and he followed. She fumbled for her keys.

"Would you prefer that I act as if it doesn't bother me that you're going out with another man?"

"Frankly, I don't care if it bothers you, because I'm going to that party and I don't need your permission." She shoved the door hard twice. It sprang open on the third push, reminding him he hadn't lubricated the lock as planned.

"So while I'm out of town, you're going on a date with him?"

Shawna swung on him. "How do I know what you're doing in Oklahoma? You could have a woman there for all I know."

"Is that what this is about? It wasn't enough when you slapped me on Friday because you're still harboring some anger, aren't you? Will it make you feel better if you hit me again? Go ahead. Hit me. I can take it."

The expression on her face suggested she was trying to decide if she should or not. "No."

"Get it out of your system," he insisted.

"Don't tempt me."

Ryan laughed shortly. "I don't think I can tempt you with anything except sex. I'm finally starting to hear you because even a blind man could see this argument is baseless. It's simply a way out for you."

"And what is it for you? You're the one making unreasonable demands."

"Maybe it's a way out for me, too." He saw something flicker in her eyes. Hurt? He wasn't sure. It could have been his imagination.

All he knew was that she didn't seem to appreciate the depth of his feelings for her and how it made him feel to know that she would be with a man she used to have feelings for—and who may still have feelings for her. He didn't care how unreasonable she thought his request.

"I think you had it right," he said. "We need to give each other space. What we had in Chicago . . . I don't know if we can recreate that." He turned away.

"Ryan."

He barely heard her, her voice was so soft. "What, Shawna? I'm giving you what you want. Space. I've made it clear to you what I want. I want *you*. Now you need to decide if you want me, too." He heaved a heavy sigh. "I know it's scary and I know I come on really strong, but it's been six years. *Six years* I've walked around like an empty shell. So you'll have to accept that it's really hard for me to slow down, and it's even harder for me to stand by and let another man interfere with what we have."

He marched down the steps and heard the door close behind him. The finality of it hit him deep in his chest. Before he entered the truck, he looked up at the next building over. Like before, someone pulled across the curtain, but he now knew it had to be Jerome because he stayed over there.

Ryan stood and stared, daring him to return to the window. When he didn't, he started his vehicle and drove out of the parking lot.

Chapter Nineteen

For days afterward, Shawna remained in a state of shock, but she managed to go about her daily routine, pretending normality. By the time a week had passed since her argument with Ryan, she'd finally stopped constantly checking her phone to see if he had called or texted.

The day of the party she was determined to participate in the festive atmosphere like all the other guests.

"This is nice," she said to Jerome. "Great view from up here."

The Benson & Gates open house party was well underway. Minutes before, she'd walked over to the window in the giant conference room at the top of the new building the firm purchased in the center of the city. The law firm used only the top four floors and leased the rest. From up here she had a good view of the Atlanta skyline spanning the night sky.

"Didn't I tell you?" Jerome asked from behind her. He wore a dark, three-piece suit and held a mixed drink in his hand.

Shawna had decided to curl her hair and sweep it to the side. The powder blue strapless dress she wore had a fitted bodice and a full chiffon skirt.

She took a good look at Jerome. "Are you having a good time?" she asked. He'd had an air of restlessness about him all night.

"To tell you the truth, I don't want to be here," he replied in a lowered voice. "I appreciate you coming to this thing with me."

"No problem. After everything you've done for me, it's the least I could do, but why don't you want to be here? It's a nice event with a good turn out."

He snorted. "I don't like coming to company parties. Before the night is over, most of these people will be drunk, and of that number, half of them will go home together."

Shawna cast a quick glance around the room. Considering the semiformal attire everyone wore, she couldn't imagine them behaving the way Jerome suggested. However, plenty of liquor floated around, and corporate parties could often get out of hand.

"Why did you come if you hate these events so much?"

He sighed. "It's good to show my face at these things, even though I don't enjoy them."

"Jerome, who's this beautiful creature with you?"

They both turned in the direction of an older man with salt and pepper hair—more salt than pepper—who had walked up. Shawna stiffened when Jerome laughed and placed his hand low on her back. The intimate gesture took her by surprise.

"This is someone very special to me. Shawna Ferguson, this is Gabe Benson."

"Nice to meet you, Mr. Benson." They shook hands.

"Call me Gabe, please." His voice boomed in the room and no one else seemed to be disturbed by it, as if they had grown accustomed to him being loud. Such a commanding voice probably worked very well in the courtroom.

"I love the table and the credenza," Shawna commented. "They look new."

"Brand spanking new," Gabe said with satisfaction. "We had them custom-made by a local craftsman." He took two steps and knocked his knuckles against the top of the table. "This is genuine mahogany, straight out of South America. It's not easy to get the real deal anymore—so many restrictions because of the depletion of the forests and all those damn illegal loggers. It cost a pretty penny, but our guy delivered and created a work of art." He couldn't have looked prouder if he'd produced the furniture himself.

"Where's Gates?" Jerome asked.

"Somewhere around here, enjoying the fact that his wife is out of town visiting the in-laws. I hope he isn't enjoying it too much." He made a drinking motion with his hand, and he and Jerome laughed. Shawna smiled, not entirely sure if laughter was appropriate.

Gabe pointed his finger at Jerome. "We have big things in store for this man right here. He's one of our hardest working attorneys."

"It's easy to work hard when you love what you do," Jerome said.

"That's what I like to hear." Gabe slapped his hands together. "Time to get some food in my body. Shawna, it was a pleasure. Jerome, don't keep her to yourself all night—let her get around to meet other people."

"Will do." Gabe patted Jerome on the shoulder and then walked away.

"He seems to really like you," Shawna said, easing out of Jerome's reach.

"I hope so. My goal is to make partner. I have big plans." He cleared his throat. "Shawna, I know we said we'd just be friends, but lately I've been thinking a lot about my future and where I hope to be in the next five years. What I'm trying to say is—"

Gabe's booming voice greeting someone caught his attention, which Shawna was happy for. The conversation had started in a direction that made her distinctly uncomfortable. She turned toward the door and had a moment of dizzying disbelief when she saw Gabe standing there with his arm around Ryan's shoulders as if they were old friends.

Ryan, in a suit.

She'd done her best to keep thoughts of him at a minimum, but his arrival made that impossible to do. He looked amazing in a black jacket, pale blue shirt, and a striped tie. Even with the stubble on his jaw, he looked polished, professional—breathtaking in a different way than he normally looked in casual attire.

A redhead stood beside him with short hair, tapered on the sides.

"Is that your friend?" Jerome asked.

Her throat muscles had tightened to the point that she could hardly breathe, and it took a while before she had the presence of mind to tear her eyes away and answer the question. "Yes, that's him."

"What's he doing here?" Jerome demanded, as if she'd violated some unspoken rule. He looked uncharacteristically upset.

"I don't know. He probably received an invitation like everyone else." Jerome looked at her with accusation in his eyes as if she'd given Ryan access to the party and sprung an unwelcome surprise on him. "I don't have anything to do with him being here. You should probably talk to Gabe about it since they seem to be friends." Jerome's hostility surprised her.

Shawna turned back to the window to pull herself together. Given their last argument, she really had no right to be jealous, but the ugly emotion rose inside her like chimney smoke.

Who was the woman with him? A friend, or more?

Ryan's image appeared as a reflection in the glass. "Good evening, Jerome. Shawna."

His voice prickled the hair on the back of her neck. Steadying her nerves, she turned slowly to face him.

"I'm surprised to see you here," Jerome said stiffly. "You know Gabe?"

"You could say that. Gabe's a great guy. We have a couple of things in common. We both grew up in farming families and it turns out he's a fellow Okie, too. I made the conference table and credenza, and he invited me to the open house." He turned his attention to Shawna even though he continued to speak to Jerome. "I hadn't planned on coming, but my plans changed at the last minute, and I decided to show up so I could take care of some business."

It was nerve-wracking the way he kept looking at her. She wished he'd stop it.

The redhead walked up beside him. "Ry, give me a couple of your business cards so I can help you hand them out."

Ry? His name contained four letters and two syllables. Was it really so difficult that she had to shorten it?

"Pardon me, I'm Jessica."

Names were exchanged and then Shawna politely asked, "What do you do?" Although she didn't feel polite. She wanted to scratch Jessica's eyes out.

Her gaze shifted to Ryan, who still stared at her. When he lowered his eyes to her bare shoulders, she experienced a sensation very much like a caress.

"I'm an interior designer," Jessica answered. "I put all of this together." She waved her hand in the general direction of the room and then plucked two cards out of a small purse.

Shawna didn't take them, leaving Jessica's hand hanging in the space between them because Ryan distracted her. The way his mouth looked.

The way his eyes remained focused on her. Too late, she realized her *faux pas*, but Jerome mitigated the awkward moment and took the cards.

"How have you been?" Ryan asked.

"Well. You?"

"Same."

"I thought you weren't coming back for a couple more days."

"I decided to cut my trip short."

The intimate tone of their voices suggested they were sequestered in a corner somewhere instead of standing in the middle of a room with dates and other guests. Shawna's pulse started an unrelenting beat in her throat. She wanted to pull him away from the other woman. She wanted to go somewhere and run her fingers through his hair, stake her claim by straddling him and peppering his skin with kisses.

Swallowing hard, her cheeks flushed with heat, Shawna lifted the hair off her neck. The room had become unbearably warm. She groaned aloud, the sound leaving her throat before she could do anything to stop it.

"You okay?" Jerome asked.

"I'm feeling a little out of it." She fanned her face. "I'm going to run to the restroom. Excuse me."

She hurried away as quickly as she could.

Chapter Twenty

Ryan scrubbed his hand across his jaw as he watched Shawna leave. He hadn't intended to come to the party even though he'd received an invitation. His family had wanted him home and he'd agreed to visit while his sister was on spring break. Unfortunately, he'd barely slept a wink in Oklahoma and had not been the best company. Over his mother's protests—and with a promise to make it up to them—he'd cut his trip short to sit at the airport on standby for hours, waiting for a flight back to Atlanta.

When he arrived at the party, Shawna had been easy to spot in a room full of dark suits and dresses because by contrast, she wore a powder-blue strapless cocktail dress. The color was striking against her beautiful dark skin and punctuated the indentation of her waist and curvature of her hips. It looked fantastic on her.

"Ryan!" Jessica's voice sounded loud and

irritated, as if she'd said his name more than once. He and Jessica had struck up a friendship about a year ago and referred business to each other from time to time. "Could you—"

"In a minute. I'll be right back." Without a backward glance at either Jessica or Jerome, Ryan set out in the same direction as Shawna.

When he found the ladies' room, he pushed the door open, not caring if he startled the women who might be inside. Enough of this nonsense about space and taking things slow. Not seeing her had simply confirmed her necessity in his life.

He walked through the sitting room and pushed the other door that took him inside the bathroom. Stopping at the entrance, he saw Shawna and another woman standing in front of the mirrored wall. The woman was washing her hands and Shawna was patting her face dry, as if she'd splashed water on it.

Her wide-eyed gaze met his in the mirror. "You can't be in here."

Again, warm tingles rippled down his back at the sound of her voice. "I came in here to talk to you." Actually, he wanted to do more than talk. He didn't plan on leaving without touching some bare part of her body. He wanted a little skin-to-skin contact.

The other woman cleared her throat and muttered an "Excuse me" before walking out.

Shawna's gaze darted to the door as it swung shut. She tossed the paper towel in the trash. "This isn't exactly the best place or time to talk."

"You'll have to adjust because I want to talk

now." He walked closer and was overcome with the need to hold her. "Jessica is a friend."

She lifted her chin. "I didn't ask you anything about her."

"You didn't have to. I know you were wondering. I told you before I'll answer any question you have. Just ask me." He hated that guarded look in her dark brown eyes. He knew the reason for it was that he'd hurt her, and she associated him with pain. He'd been miserable the past week and a half without any contact between them, but how did she feel? "I missed you."

Her gaze lowered, her long lashes shielding her eyes and hiding whatever she didn't want him to see.

She moistened her lips with her tongue and his groin tightened at the slow movement.

"Shawna," he groaned, stepping closer.

She moved backward as he heard the outer door swing open. Someone else was about to enter, and he still hadn't gotten the answer to the question uppermost in his mind: did she want to be with him or not?

Quickly, he looped his arm around her waist and pulled her behind the louvered door of the first bathroom stall. The narrow space didn't afford much room to maneuver.

The laughter and conversation of two females filled the bathroom. He didn't let Shawna go, holding her close. The heat of her body seeped through the jacket and shirt and warmed his skin underneath. His breathing quickened as she pressed her palms against his chest.

"What are you doing?" she whispered.

"Holding you," he replied.

They listened as both women used the facilities. Ryan kept his eyes trained on her, but she avoided his gaze, looking at everything except him as an erection slowly hardened in his pants.

Minutes later, two toilets flushed and then he could hear the voices of the women again. Unable to withstand it any longer, he lowered his head to Shawna's temptingly bare neck and took a slow drag. The scent of some floral bouquet swirled up his nostrils and almost made him groan. With his free hand he caressed the bare skin of one shoulder and trailed it up to the back of her neck. He thumbed the silky strands at the edge of her hairline.

Shawna inhaled sharply and the sound urged him to kiss the corner of her mouth.

She shivered in his arms. "Ryan, stop." The voices faded as the women left them alone. "What do you want?"

"You know what I want." He reached one hand up to cup her face, but she knocked it down and pushed him away.

"Don't touch me. I don't even want to see you."

He gave her a measured look. "Who's the liar now, Shawna?"

"You're pretty confident. How do you know—" His fingertip brushed her lips, and she broke off her tirade with a gasp.

"That's how I know," Ryan said.

Shawna blinked rapidly and swallowed. "I hate the way you make me feel. Hate it."

"You think I like this?" Ryan asked. "You think I like being obsessed with you? I hate it, too. I hate this power you have over me. The only thing I hate more is being without you."

Her bottom lip quivered. "You hate being without me so much that you *left*." She pushed him hard. Her shove did little to move him, but he stepped back anyway and braced his back against the wall.

"I did that for you. To give you time to think."

"*You left me*." She pounded his chest with her fists.

He didn't stop her because he understood she needed to get it out. He took the blows, standing there, looking down at her. "No."

"Yes." She stopped punching him and stepped back, chest heaving.

"No."

"*Yes*." She came at him again, but this time, instead of attacking him, she grabbed his head and slammed her mouth over his.

It startled him at first and he froze, but it didn't take him long to recover. When his senses returned, he wrapped his arms around her and drew her up on her toes with a firm hold. He pushed her into the opposite wall, holding on tight and devouring her mouth, dragging groans of pleasure from her.

"Over a week," he said against her mouth. He was already out of control, the way she always made him feel. "For over a week I haven't seen you. I haven't touched you. I haven't smelled you."

He latched onto her lips again, his tongue

pushing its way between them to steal her sweetness. Shawna guided his hand under her dress, and Ryan slid it across her bare derriere. She moaned, and he grew harder hearing those breathy little noises she made.

When his fingers went in search of the heat between her legs, she pushed away his hand before it reached its goal. "Wait."

The tip of his thumb lined the seam of her lips to silence her. Her eyes darkened to a sultry hue, and her lips parted for him, exposing her irregular breathing.

"We can't do this here. Not like this," she said in a shaky voice.

"Then stop me." He tasted her lips again. They were bruised and swollen.

"I can't," she whispered.

"I can't stop, either," he whispered back.

Can't. Not won't, but *can't*. There was a certain inevitability about it. A resignation to an inescapable fact. Incapable. Unable to do otherwise. *Can't*. He kissed her again, his muscular body straining against hers while prodding her lips to yield to the press of his tongue.

Her ears buzzed from the manner in which he now used both hands to shove her dress up over her thighs to her hips. The lightweight fabric pooled across his forearms before he slid his fingers slowly, torturously, beneath the flimsy sheer panties she wore.

One hand found its way between her legs and her body sang under each masterful stroke. His fingers slid between the folds, coaxing more moisture from her and playing with her pebbled clit in such a way that made her thighs tighten and her legs shake from the sensual power of his touch. He'd become considerably harder and longer as their kiss deepened and their caresses became more frantic. She could feel every solid inch of him and her stomach clenched in need.

His mouth traveled down her throat, the tip of his tongue licking the soft skin at the top of her bodice. Her fingers tunneled into his satiny dark hair, anchoring him to her. She sighed with satisfaction at being so close to him again. Thousands of invisible needles of desire pricked the surface of her skin where the coarse stubble on his chin and jaw grazed the swollen crests of her breasts.

The zipper on her dress lowered and the top fell away. Ryan paused for a moment, his harsh breath showering the exposed skin with warmth.

"Please," she whispered, cupping her breasts and offering them to him.

They were extremely sensitive and the tips tightened to stinging peaks. She was so far gone she no longer cared about where they were; she wanted relief. He obliged, but barely, choosing only to flick his tongue across one dark peak. She begged him for more, pleaded. Finally, he covered the nipple and areola with his mouth, sucking until she helplessly moaned into his hair as she clutched him.

He lifted his head so his mouth could devour hers again. Then her neck. Then her collarbone. Kissing, nipping, sucking.

He dragged her underwear past her knees. She

stepped out of them while he undid his pants. After slamming down the lid on the commode, he sat down and fit a condom over his distended shaft.

Legs trembling, Shawna stood before him.

What had happened to her? Who had he made her become? This wanton with no inhibitions. Hot sex the first night they met, against the wall in an alley, and now this. Anytime, anywhere Ryan wanted her she was accessible to him.

He tugged her hand and pulled her between his legs. His eyes bored into her as he waited, letting her make the next move. It was her decision how far they would go.

Slowly, she lifted her skirt, and his nostrils flared as he watched her movements. The material gathered around her thighs and she climbed on, sinking onto his turgid flesh, letting his heat fill her. A tortured groan filled the small enclosure. Shawna had no idea if the sound came from him or her, but it embodied everything she felt inside—a need for him that was borderline painful.

Arms wound around his neck, she writhed on his hips in sweet agony. More kisses, breathless, hungry. Ragged breaths expelled from their lungs with the urgency of their desire. His hands tightened on the flesh of her bottom and her moans became louder as she edged toward release.

"Wrap your legs around me, love," he said, his voice dark and low. "Let me get in there good."

She did as he instructed, crossing her ankles high on his back. He leaned forward, swelling, going even deeper. "That's it," he rasped, his jaw tight. "Ah, you feel so good. I missed you."

She couldn't tear her eyes away, caught in his gaze, their connection deep and profound.

With his hand braced against the wall and one strong arm supporting her back, Ryan shifted them into a forty-five degree angle. He surged inside of her. The shoes slipped from her elevated feet and clattered to the floor, but it didn't stop their frenzied pumping.

Her head fell back as she abandoned herself to the sexual rhythm. The ceiling light swirled with each thrust of his hips. She felt the gentle rasp of his tongue as it took turns on each of her nipples before he sucked one between his lips. The sensitive flesh throbbed with each protracted pull of his mouth, and she closed her eyes to savor the fiery sensations he ignited across her skin and through her veins.

Suddenly, her whole body exploded like a series of grenades had been detonated. Crying out in a strangled voice, Shawna's entire body tightened around him like a vice. The aftershocks rippled through her in a powerful wave.

Ryan crushed her against him. His hand fisted at her back as he climaxed right behind her, letting loose a primal groan into the curls swept to the side of her head.

Their harsh breathing couldn't drown out the sound of high heels on the tile, and the door swinging shut penetrated the afterglow. Someone had just left. They'd been so entrenched in their lovemaking they hadn't heard anyone enter.

Shawna placed her feet on the floor as Ryan

straightened on the seat. She gently brushed the damp hair from his temple and ran her fingers along the back of his neck and upper back. She rubbed his shoulders, pressed her nose to the collar of his shirt and closed her eyes. He smelled so good. A mixture of sweat, cologne, and man.

"I missed you, too," she whispered. "I'm sorry."

"There's nothing to be sorry about. We both said things we shouldn't have. Nothing matters but right now. We'll keep the past in the past."

She kissed his rough jaw. "Don't leave me again."

"I won't. I promise."

Chapter Twenty-one

Although Shawna wanted to slink away from prying eyes, she and Ryan agreed they owed Jerome and Jessica the courtesy of an in-person goodbye.

They did what they could to fix their clothes, but she had no doubt anyone who took a look at them would know what they'd done in the bathroom stall. Their clothes were wrinkled and their faces flushed. And no matter how much she tried, nothing she did could revive her limp curls.

If their general appearance didn't tip off the average observer, Ryan's hand fastened around hers provided another clue. It was a territorial move, and it made a statement that she may have arrived with someone else, but they were leaving together because she was his. Not that she minded. Her fingers curled tightly around his, too, staking her own claim as she stayed close to his side.

Their eyes searched the room. Shawna spotted Jessica and they walked over to say goodbye. Ryan offered his friend cab fare, which she declined. She made a remark about not having to be concerned about getting a ride home and then suggestively cast her eyes in the direction of one of the attorneys standing near the window speaking to two other people. The man lifted a corner of his mouth in a flirtatious smile at her before resuming his conversation.

Ignoring the elevated brows of Gabe Benson—whose eyes didn't miss the handholding—Ryan and Shawna said goodbye and thanked him for his hospitality. They waited around for a while and searched a few other rooms, but they never did see Jerome again.

After some prodding, Shawna agreed they should leave. Jessica promised to let Jerome know they were gone whenever he made an appearance.

Outside in the chilly air, Ryan removed his jacket and draped it over Shawna's shoulders. "You're not dressed for this weather."

"I'm a woman. I'm used to suffering for fashion."

He shook his head, and it made her happy to see the lazy smile back in place. "Where to?"

"My place," she suggested.

They climbed into the truck and she slid across the seat to rest her head on his shoulder. "I can't drive like this," Ryan complained good-naturedly.

Shawna wrapped her arm around his chest. "Figure it out, because I'm not moving." Now that he was back, she resolved to stay close to his side.

"Demanding woman," he said, putting his arm around her. He squeezed her tight, relishing the feel of her in his arms. Then he kissed the top of her head and pulled out of the parking lot.

****

Ryan and Shawna drifted in and out of sleep, whispering to each other and telling silly jokes. The last time he had awakened her with his erection prodding her thighs and his hands cupping her breasts. When they finished with a short, passionate bout of lovemaking, they'd fallen asleep with him still inside of her, their bodies curled into a semicircle.

The dull whir of a telephone caused Shawna to wake up. She nudged Ryan with her elbow. "That's your phone."

He didn't like having his sleep disturbed. He rolled away onto his back with a groan, and she immediately missed his warmth and the intimacy of their connected body parts.

The vibrating phone continued to buzz and he hopped off the bed to grab it from his jacket pocket. "Hello?"

She watched his naked silhouette against the window, wondering who could be calling at this hour. She heard him curse, say a few curt words, and then end with, "I'll be right there."

Shawna sat up and turned on the lamp beside the bed. "What's wrong?"

"Someone broke into the shop." He started putting on his clothes.

"Oh, no. Did they take anything?"

"Fortunately, no. The police arrived in time to stop them. Two teenagers, they said."

"Do you want me to come with you?" she asked.

"No, it shouldn't take long. They rammed their truck through the front entrance, so the police need me to come down there to secure the building and answer some questions."

"What would they want in your workshop?"

"They may have planned to steal some of my tools, machinery, the computers, or the software I use for my design work. It could be anything." He slipped on his second shoe and walked over to her side of the bed.

Shawna pouted. "Hurry back."

"I will." He cupped her face and gave her kiss.

When his mouth lingered, she started to giggle and pushed him away. "Go."

"Oh yeah, I forgot what I was supposed to be doing." With one last kiss, he rushed out the door.

After he left, Shawna slid down into the bed to catch some sleep until he came back. Thinking about the next day, she realized she didn't have any food to make breakfast in the morning. She looked at her cell phone screen to check the time. Despite the hour, the store a mile or so down the road would be open. If she hurried, she could pick up a few items before they closed.

She made a mental list while she dressed and left the house shortly after Ryan. When she returned, she had a plastic bag with eggs, milk, juice, and bread.

She made her way slowly up the steps onto her dark porch. With her head bent, she wriggled the key into the doorknob and unlocked the door.

Now the deadbolt. She twisted it to the right and pushed once. It didn't budge. She really needed to get this fixed. She twisted and pushed again. Nothing. *Come on, come on.*

She was about to push again when someone grabbed from behind. With a cry, she dropped the plastic bag filled with groceries, and it landed on the porch with a *thunk* as large hands spun her around and pushed backward. Her head hit the door so hard she saw stars.

"Cheating slut." *Cheating?* It was Jerome, and he smelled like he'd downed a bottle of vodka. "Not good enough for you? I'm an attorney, but you'd rather be with a damn *furniture maker?*" he asked.

Shawna shrank back against the door. He didn't touch her again, but he didn't allow her to move, either. He crowded her with a menacing posture.

"Answer the question."

"I don't know what you're—"

"Did you have sex with him?" he sneered.

Unsure how to answer, her heart started a wild thumping. "I don't know what—"

"Don't lie. I know you did." His heavily slurred speech frightened her. She didn't know what he would do in this state, and he had the advantage in size and strength.

She slipped a hand inside the open mouth of her purse, careful not to make a sudden move and draw attention to her action. She didn't have pepper spray, but she had menthol mouth spray somewhere in there, which she planned to turn into a weapon to defend herself if she needed to.

"One of the paralegals said she heard two people having sex in the bathroom," Jerome continued. "Since you and Ryan were missing, it didn't take a genius to figure out who were the culprits. Then you left together." He shook his head and laughed bitterly. "I can't believe how long I've waited for you. I've helped you lug groceries, I helped you change a flat on that raggedy car you drove. When it gave you problems, I volunteered to take you anywhere you needed to go and never took a dime from you for gas money. I thought you were special. I thought you were a different kind of woman. I treated you like a queen and put you on a pedestal, but women like you don't appreciate a man like me."

Shawna remained silent, worried that anything she said would set him off. She could count on one hand the number of times she'd asked for any of those favors, and he'd refused to take money from her. He'd always been there to help and she'd accepted, but he'd had an ulterior motive all along.

Her fingers found the spray and she thumbed off the cover.

"Two years," Jerome said, holding up two digits. "And you let a man you barely know fuck you in the bathroom at my company's office party like a whore. While you were there with me, you fucking slut."

"I'm not a—"

"You're a slut!" he said louder, getting in her face.

She held her breath and angled her head away

from the stench of his mouth, tightening her fingers around the vial. Fighting back the tremors that threatened to overtake her, she found her voice. "Step back."

His face twisted into an ugly snarl. "Don't worry. I'm not foolish enough to harm you. I value my career and won't jeopardize it over you."

He dipped his head to look her in the eye. "You think he's going to make a commitment to you? Men don't make commitments to women who are easy."

"You don't know what you're talking about," Shawna said in a small voice.

"I know exactly what I'm talking about. What you did was disgusting." He laughed shortly. "When he dumps you, don't call me because I don't want another man's leftovers. And I don't like sluts and that's what you are—a filthy slut. I refuse to dirty my hands with you." He looked at her with disgust, as if she was something nasty.

Then he turned around and walked off the porch.

Chapter Twenty-two

Ryan returned to Shawna's house, whistling as he went up the walkway.

Boarding up the building had taken longer than expected. The teens had broken in the double doors, and the impact of the crash caused structural damage to one wall. He'd had to call one of his employees who lived nearby to help him.

He ran up the steps and took out his phone to call Shawna to let him in when he noted the plastic bag near the door. He picked it up and dialed her number.

"Hi, I'm outside. So are your groceries," he added with amusement. "You're too young to be this forgetful already."

"I'll be right there."

Hearing the sullen tone of her voice, he became instantly alert. "What's the matter?" he asked sharply.

"Nothing. I'm coming down to get you."

Moments later, Shawna let him into the dark entryway. Seeing her shapely form outlined beneath the silk robe should have captured his attention and spiked his libido, but it didn't. What caught his attention was her lack of response to his arrival and how she avoided looking at him.

"Thanks," she said in a hoarse voice. She reached for the bag, still keeping her eyes averted and using her hair as a cover.

"What's wrong?"

"I said nothing."

Ryan flipped the switch on the wall. She squinted against the bright light and covered her face.

"Look at me." He dropped the bag on the side table and took her chin in his hand. "You've been crying," he said, noting her reddened eyes.

Shawna pulled away from him. "I'm fine."

"You're not. What happened between the time I left and now? I thought we were good."

Backing away even more, she crossed her arms over her waist. Neither of them spoke as they looked at each other. Ryan didn't know why she was behaving this way, but it pained him to watch her distance herself from him.

"This isn't normal."

He didn't have to ask her to explain. She meant their relationship. "Says who?"

"I want normal."

"No, you don't. Normal is boring. This is way more exciting."

She gave a humorless laugh. "You have an answer for everything."

"I wish I did. Then I'd know what to say to put your mind at ease." He moved to reach out to her, but she tightened her arms around herself.

She blinked rapidly and gazed up at the ceiling before looking at him again. "In Chicago, I suspected that you'd lied to me."

He frowned. "What are you talking about?"

"I suspected that you might be involved with someone."

"How?"

"I just did. That first night at the restaurant, when I asked you if you had a girlfriend, I suspected you weren't completely honest. I wondered if you were lying to me when you said your brother called the next morning, too. I could have asked you more questions, but I was afraid to know the answers."

"I remember the look in your eyes when you saw me with Holly. You have no idea how much it killed me to know I caused that pain." He ran his fingers through his hair. The hurt he'd caused her had lashed his conscience. "I thought we agreed to keep the past in the past. Six years ago doesn't matter. We're starting fresh, here, now. No distractions."

It's true they'd agreed to that, but the confrontation with Jerome had left her shaken and ashamed. She continued speaking as if he hadn't said anything. "When I saw you with her, I felt so used. Like I was nothing to you," she whispered.

"You weren't nothing."

"Being with you like that was the only time in my entire life that I had ever done anything remotely spontaneous. The *one* time I threw caution to the wind, I ended up on the wrong side of a love triangle."

"Shawna—"

"Let me finish." She took a deep breath. "It's not that I don't believe you care about me. I'm past that and I do believe you. You've shown me that you do. But I'm afraid all this passion and intensity will fade and then you'll realize that you made a mistake. What if you meet someone else the way you met me? Then you won't want *me* anymore, and I'll be alone with this ache inside of me that won't go away. So how do I know that won't happen again? How do *you* know?"

He looked at her as if she was crazy. "Because I love you, Shawna." He said the sentence in such a way that the question *How could you even ask me that?* was implied. No hesitation on his part, no awkwardness. The words sounded natural, as if it had always been—never mentioned, but understood.

He came closer. "I think I fell in love with you the moment you smiled at me as we walked down Michigan Avenue. My feelings for you are real. I've never been surer of anything in my life. It doesn't matter to me that we've only had a few days together because you make me happy like no one else. I've never loved anyone the way I love you, and I know I never will again."

She inhaled, suddenly aware that she'd been holding her breath for the latter part of his speech. Only now did she realize she'd been waiting for him to say those words—had *needed* to hear him say them. "I love you, too."

He took one of her hands in his and drew her in, their faces close together. "You're right, what's between us isn't normal. It's better than normal. We can't do normal. We just have to do us."

Us.

"I don't want to go through life without you," he said softly.

"I don't want to go through life without you, either." Her fingers stroked his jaw. "I couldn't bear it."

****

Ryan sat in his truck outside Shawna's building. At the moment, she and her staff worked at La Petite Robe, doing inventory and preparing for a weekend event where a local designer with a name he couldn't pronounce would arrive to promote pieces from her line.

Shawna expected members of the media to be in attendance, and her best clients would go to the store early to rub elbows with the designer and get previews of the full collection. He'd promised to go by later and help her with anything she needed, even if only to move furniture around. He had to take care of this one little thing first, and now was the perfect time to do it while she was occupied at the store.

Last night, he'd cupped the back of her head and felt a bump there, and that's when she'd told him the details of what happened between her and Jerome. He'd been furious. At Jerome, and even at himself for not fixing that damn deadbolt like he'd planned to. He'd been ready to go next door to Jerome's townhouse, but she'd begged him not to.

"It's not worth it. I'm fine," she'd said, holding onto him when he'd charged toward the door. "Come upstairs with me. Wouldn't you rather do that than go over there and confront him?" When he didn't respond, she'd continued. "Please, let it go. For me? Don't do anything stupid."

He'd responded that he wouldn't, and he hadn't exactly lied to her. Yes, he'd promised not to do anything stupid, but this wasn't stupid. This was the logical result of someone putting their hands on the woman he loved and causing her physical and emotional pain. He couldn't let Jerome get away with what he'd done.

When a black BMW rolled by, he watched its progress in the rearview mirror. Jerome had arrived.

Ryan exited the truck. When he'd arrived earlier, he'd loosened the bulb on Jerome's porch, darkening it in heavy shadows. Moving quickly and quietly, he was up on Jerome's porch before the man even knew he followed him. By then it was too late.

He began to turn, but Ryan twisted his arm behind his back and grabbed his neck, shoving his face into the door.

Jerome began to sputter and shake. "Who—what—"

"Be quiet."

"Ryan?"

"That's right."

"What the hell?"

"Stop moving or I'll break your arm."

A tremor passed through Jerome and he closed his eyes.

"Open your eyes." He flicked them back open and Ryan's voice hardened with the effort it took to keep himself in check. "We Oklahoma boys don't like it when someone threatens our women."

"I didn't threaten—"

"Shut up." Ryan pulled Jerome's arm higher up his back and heard him whimper. "You may not have come right out and said the words, but you most certainly threatened her when you sneaked up on her in the dark the way you did. Kind of like what I did to you. Do you feel threatened?" When he didn't answer, Ryan repeated the question louder and squeezed his neck. "Do you feel threatened?"

"Yes, yes. Yes, I do."

Ryan loosened his grip on Jerome's neck enough so that his cheek no longer pressed into the door, but he kept his arm in the same awkward position. "Here's what's going to happen. You're going to leave Shawna alone. Don't speak to her. Don't even look in her direction again. Do you understand?"

"Do you realize I could have you arrested? I'm an attorney. I could sue you, destroy your reputation—anything I choose."

Ryan had to hand it to Jerome; he had balls. "I don't care what your profession is. Matter of fact, I happen to know a really good attorney, too. You may have heard of him—Gabe Benson, your boss. Turns out, we have a lot in common. I wonder what he'd think about your behavior, considering you've probably been kissing his ass for years trying to move up in his firm."

Jerome's lips tightened and he remained silent.

"So let me ask you using lawyer-speak so there's no confusion," Ryan said. "Do you understand the terms under which you're to perform in your revised relationship with Shawna?"

"Yes."

"Lucky for you that college-educated brain of yours kicked in and helped you make the right decision." Ryan patted him on the back in a condescending manner. "I'm glad we understand each other. Next time, pick on someone your own size."

Ryan turned away, but his instincts warned him what kind of man Jerome would be, and he was right. He'd hoped Jerome would take a shot at him so he'd have an excuse to hit him. As the other man swung, he dodged. Moving quickly, Ryan landed a right hook that jerked Jerome's head back. He staggered backward and Ryan followed, landing a left jab to his midsection and another blow to the face that sent him crashing into the wall. He slid to the floor in a daze, blood trickling from his left nostril.

"Come on," Ryan said, pacing restlessly. Adrenalin pumped through his veins. He was more than ready to go toe-to-toe with this guy. It couldn't be over already.

"Get away from me," Jerome whimpered, flinging his arms over his head.

Ryan's fisted hand itched to land another punch, but he refrained. Jerome cowered on the floor of the porch. Like all bullies, he toppled when someone stood up to him.

Disgusted, Ryan left without another word.

****

When Ryan arrived at La Petite Robe, Shawna and her staff were in the midst of setting up. They'd moved the clothing racks to create a runway down the middle of the store and set chairs along the length of it. One staff member was in the process of placing brochures and other literature on a table, while another dressed the mannequins in the visiting designer's outfits.

"Where do you need me?" Ryan asked.

Shawna looked closely at him. "What took you so long?"

"I had something to take care of."

Her gaze ran down his arm and rested on the reddened and bruised knuckles of his hand. "What happened?" she asked in a lowered voice so her employees couldn't hear. "You didn't do anything crazy, did you?"

"Nothing crazy. I guess you could say I hit something."

"Something or *someone*?"

He shrugged.

"Ryan, you promised."

"I only promised I wouldn't do anything stupid."

"What if he calls the police?"

"He won't. It doesn't matter anyway, because I'd do the same thing a hundred more times and go to jail each time. I had to make sure he understood if he ever hurts you again, he'll have to deal with me."

The look of worry ebbed from her features. Her eyes softened. "What am I going to do with you?"

"Keep me."

She bit her bottom lip. "Did you get him good?"

He chuckled. "Yeah."

Her face broadened into a grin. "Good."

Ryan looked around. "All right, what do you need me to do?" he asked, halfway turning away from her to assess the work that needed to be done.

Shawna took his arm and pulled him back around to face her. She rose up onto her toes and kissed him lightly on the mouth. "Thank you."

Her staff whistled and made kissing noises. "Get back to work," she said.

When they did, she kissed him again.

Epilogue

One year later

Paris Fashion Week wrapped up days ago, but Ryan and Shawna still had three more days in Paris.

In the beginning, she'd managed to get him into a couple of the less restricted venues to see the unveiling of the designers' collections. When he dozed off during one of the runway shows, she told him he didn't have to suffer through any more events. At first he insisted it wouldn't happen again, but she'd finally gotten him to admit that he'd rather drink turpentine than see another designer outfit.

Armed with a book of common English-to-French phrases and lots of advice from Shawna, he explored the city on his own while she went to meetings and attended industry shows.

They paid an exorbitant fee to stay at their

particular hotel on perhaps the best-known avenue in the world, the Champs-Élysées. Shawna's first visit to Paris had involved much more modest accommodations, but they'd both agreed that it was worth the splurge to have a good time and create new memories together.

"Oui, oui. Je sais, mais j'étais occupée. Et ce soir, Ryan et moi, nous allons sortir. Demain, je viendrai là, je te promets. Gros bisous. Muah."

Shawna hung up the phone. Tomorrow they'd visit some of her old friends, including her former landlord who owned the bakery she'd lived above years ago. She'd just apologized for not coming by sooner and told him she would stop by tomorrow. Tonight she and Ryan planned to have dinner at one of the fine dining restaurants within walking distance.

"This one or this one?" Ryan held up two ties against his white shirt.

Shawna pointed to the one on the right with a black and blue grid pattern. "That one, and wear the blue shirt."

"I'm pretty sure I knew how to dress before I met you," he said with a frown.

Shawna wrinkled her nose. "Barely." She bent to slip on her shoes.

"What was that?" He grabbed her from behind and she screeched. "I got you though, didn't I?" he said into the crook of her neck.

"Yes, you did."

With one arm still around her, he lifted her left hand. The three diamonds in her engagement band reflected the light and glimmered on her finger. He'd proposed the night before during a romantic candlelit dinner.

She hadn't had a chance to tell her sister yet. As she watched Ryan get dressed in the blue shirt and tie she'd suggested, she decided now was as good a time as any and picked up the phone. She walked over to the window to gaze out at the night.

"What time is it there?" Yvonne asked after they'd greeted each other.

"A little after seven. We're about to go out to dinner." Her ten-month-old nephew bellowed in the background. "What's he hollering about?"

"He's being greedy. Hang on a sec, let me give him his bottle." Moments later, the loud screams stopped. "Whew. He is the greediest little thing."

Although her sister sounded exhausted, Shawna knew she was happy. "I called to tell you my good news. I couldn't hold it anymore."

"What's that?"

"Ryan proposed."

Yvonne screamed, which made Shawna pull the phone away from her ear. "He did?"

"Yes, he did."

Yvonne sighed. "An engagement in Paris. How romantic."

"I guess I'll be joining the ranks of the married and crazy soon. Then the kids will follow." Her stomach tilted sideways at the thought of carrying Ryan's babies.

"You'll love it. I personally love being a full-time mommy, but you'll have to find your own balance with your business and the kids. You probably have a flow chart already created, don't you?" Before she could answer the teasing question, Yvonne followed up with another. "How'd he do on the ring?"

"He did a good job," she replied, stretching her fingers in front of her to admire it.

"I knew I liked him," Yvonne said. "I can't wait to see it."

"I never did thank you, did I?"

"For what?"

Shawna looked over her shoulder. Ryan stood in front of the mirror slipping on his jacket. "For setting me up on that blind date."

"I'll take the credit, but I'm sure if I didn't, Ryan would have devised some other plan to get to you."

"Probably, but I'm glad you did it anyway. That night changed everything. My life hasn't been the same since."

"I'm so happy for you."

"Thanks. I better go. I wanted to say hi and tell you my good news. Say hi to William and kiss the kids for me."

Shawna hung up and walked over to Ryan to straighten his tie. "There," she said.

"I'm presentable now?" he asked.

His mouth tilted up in the smile that had won her over from day one. The blue of the shirt brought out the color of his eyes; the main reason she'd wanted him to wear it.

"Yes," she answered, rising up on her toes to kiss his lips. "Love you." She swiped lipstick from his mouth with her thumb.

"Say it in French," he whispered.

"Je t'aime, mon amour."

He groaned and then smiled. He liked it when she spoke French. "Love you, too, future Mrs. Stewart."

Minutes later, they left the hotel to go to dinner, and strolled hand in hand down the Champs-Élysées.

The End

More Stories by Delaney Diamond

Hot Latin Men series
The Arrangement
Fight for Love
Private Acts
Second Chances
Hot Latin Men: Vol. I (print anthology)
Hot Latin Men: Vol. II (print anthology)

Hawthorne Family series
The Temptation of a Good Man
A Hard Man to Love
Here Comes Trouble
For Better or Worse
Hawthorne Family Series: Vol. I (print anthology)
Hawthorne Family Series: Vol. II (print anthology)

Love Unexpected series
The Blind Date
The Wrong Man

Bailar series (sweet/clean romance)
Worth Waiting For

Short Story
Subordinate Position
The Ultimate Merger

Free Stories
www.delaneydiamond.com

About the Author

Delaney Diamond is the bestselling author of sweet and sensual romance novels. Originally from the U.S. Virgin Islands, she now lives in Atlanta, Georgia. She has been an avid reader for as long as she can remember and in her spare time reads romance novels, mysteries, thrillers, and a fair amount of non-fiction.

When she's not busy reading or writing, she's in the kitchen trying out new recipes, dining at one of her favorite restaurants, or traveling to an interesting locale. She speaks fluent conversational French and can get by in Spanish. You can enjoy free reads and the first chapter of all her novels on her website.

Join her distribution list to get notices about new releases.

http://delaneydiamond.com
https://www.facebook.com/DelaneyDiamond

CPSIA information can be obtained at www.ICGtesting.com
Printed in the USA
LVOW08s1449190814

399899LV00001B/37/P